"You're not w... ring, Ellen."

"You were out of town," she said, repeating the story she'd fabricated. "We became engaged long-distance. There was no chance to get a ring."

Josh tilted his head in acquiescence. "Yes, but I'm back now." He popped open a black velvet box to reveal an exquisite diamond ring.

Ellen stared at the ring, then at Josh. "It's lovely, but I can't accept it. And what will you do with it once this ruse is over? Someday you'll want to marry. Are you going to give your fiancée a slightly used ring?"

"Don't worry. I have no plans to get married. I was thinking you might like to keep it—as a souvenir."

"No." When all this was over, she didn't want any reminders. Because the fact was that Josh and this stage they'd created was a fantasy, only an illusion. And Ellen knew firsthand what happened to people who tried to make their daydreams come to life—and failed.

Myrna Mackenzie has always been fascinated by the belief that within every man is a hero, inside every woman lives a heroine. She loves to write about ordinary people making extraordinary dreams come true. A former teacher, Myrna lives in the suburbs of Chicago with her husband—who was her high-school sweetheart—and her two sons. Readers can write to Myrna at PO Box 225, LaGrange, IL 60525-0225 USA.

Recent titles by the same author:

THE BABY WISH

THE SECRET GROOM

BY
MYRNA MACKENZIE

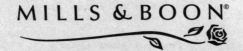

To Margaret, who understands where words come from. When I went looking for a writers' group, I never expected to find a great friend, too. Thanks for always being a phone call away.

First published in Great Britain 2000
Harlequin Mills & Boon Limited,
Eton House, 18-24 Paradise Road, Richmond, Surrey TW9 1SR

© Myrna Topol 1997

ISBN 0 263 81977 9

Set in Times Roman 10½ on 12 pt.
01-0004-52386

Printed and bound in Spain
by Litografia Rosés, S.A., Barcelona

Chapter One

"If I had a man like that waiting for me at home, I'd never leave the house again...not even to go get chocolate."

"Uh-uh. Not for anything. I'd just buy the biggest bed I could find and set up camp there—for life."

Ellen Rhoades stopped dead just inside the doorway of the central office of Tarenton Toys. Her lunch hour was over and there was a crowd of women standing around her desk studying the photo of Josh Hawthorne she'd placed there that morning.

No question, the man looked like every woman's midnight fantasy. Had she really had the nerve to announce that she was now engaged to Josh? Thank goodness no one had actually ever met the man. They'd know inside two seconds that she'd lied. Josh had never been a one-woman man any more than she had ever been a marriage-minded woman—but on him it showed. One look at that sensual grin, the purposeful roll to his shoulders when he moved, and everyone would know that this man lived only to pursue life's pleasures. Josh didn't have a serious cell in his body and he barely knew Ellen Rhoades, hadn't laid eyes on her in years. But of course, that was why she had chosen him.

Forced to the proverbial, professional wall, Ellen had finally admitted that no matter how qualified she was, how hard she worked, her career was stymied if she didn't play the Tarenton game and espouse the happy-family image. She loved this place. She delighted in knowing her job brought joy to children everywhere and she hated lying to her associates, nearly choked on every word. But the truth was that she needed a fiancé, a mate—for the short-term, anyway. So Josh, safely out of sight, consulting with some wealthy legal clients in Europe for the next few months, had seemed like the perfect pretend fiancé.

Still, watching her co-workers salivating over the picture of a bare-chested Josh, Ellen wondered if she hadn't made a tactical error. Maybe that photo *had* been a bad choice. Perhaps it *was* a bit too sensual. She wanted her boss to envision her as June Cleaver—not an insatiable love slave living out an X-rated fantasy.

"Ms. Rhoades, I'd like to have a word with you."

That bullfrog croak was too distinctive for Ellen to imagine that it belonged to anyone other than her boss. Closing her eyes for two seconds and taking a deep, enervating breath, Ellen turned, aiming for calmness, a confident smile. She nodded toward Mr. Tarenton's office, one of the few walled spaces in the wide-open room, but the portly man frowned and shook his head.

"Out here will do." He led the way toward her desk, scattering the ladies like pale and silent bowling pins.

Ellen felt an uncharacteristic urge to panic and throw her body over that photo. Chances were good that Mr.

Tarenton hadn't yet seen the picture of Josh. If she could stall him, everything would be fine.

She'd spent the last three weeks playing the game, had sent herself candy and gifts, all supposedly from Josh. The fact that the man was her former college roommate's ex-boyfriend, and that he and Penny were still friends who kept in touch, made him perfect. Ellen knew he was out of the country. She had photos, stories she'd heard. But that picture—well, damn Josh Hawthorne for having sexy, amber eyes, for looking like what he was: a man who saw life as a game with no rules. Wealthy, carefree Josh had always seemed amused when Ellen insisted on spending her Friday nights studying. Now, without even being here, she could imagine him grinning at her careful efforts to control her career. She should have anticipated this problem, realized that Mr. Tarenton would take one look at Josh and think "male centerfold" rather than "family man." What had possessed her to think otherwise? Why had she chosen Josh? Penny had plenty of other ex-boyfriends.

Sailing into her best executive glide, Ellen smiled at Mr. Tarenton and breezed toward her desk, all business as she rustled a stack of papers, delicately flipping the framed photo facedown with her other hand.

Mr. Tarenton let out a rolling chuckle. "I don't blame you for being so proprietary with that one, Ellen. He's a hell of a handsome devil. You've got all the men around here sucking their guts in and the women smiling to themselves. I just wanted to tell you that I approve completely. You're one of my most valuable employees, and this is damn good news, you tying the knot."

Ellen wanted to close her eyes in relief, to send up a prayer of thanks. She wanted to kiss Josh Hawthorne's glass-plated lips, call Penny and thank her for lending her that photo. Instead she simply picked up the frame, dusting it off as she turned to her boss. "Thank you, Mr. Tarenton. I appreciate your taking an interest in me. I've always enjoyed working here. Tarenton Toys is like a second home to me."

Mr. Tarenton's chuckle became a guffaw. "And don't I know it? When I hired you seven years ago, you were this quiet little thing, worked so hard you couldn't have even had time to date. I was beginning to think you'd never get married."

Ellen looked up at her boss, smiling weakly as she pushed a strand of straight brown hair back over her shoulder. "Oh, well, me, too," she managed to say. "I've just been so very involved with the company, and I've been working on some new ideas that..."

"I know, I know. You're a wonderful asset to this business, Ellen. But marriage, family, that's what Tarenton Toys is really all about," he said, banging his palm on her desk. "Marriage is what makes the world go 'round. Don't you agree?"

She didn't. Her parents' marriage had been a mistake that ended in their neglecting their children. Her baby sister was in the middle of a divorce right now and suffering terribly. Holding Lynn close and letting her sob the way she had when they were kids, how could she embrace her supervisor's credo?

"Marriage is an important institution," Ellen conceded. *But for the Rhoades women, marriage meant only pain and disappointment. So it wasn't for everyone—definitely not for her. She had a challenging career instead, one she truly enjoyed. It was the way she wanted things.*

Her boss nodded, waving his other hand around. "Look at this, every top-level executive married. That's Tarenton Toys. People settling down, having children, closing books. Must be almost the end of the day.

It had been a good day, all things considered. Mr. Tarenton had still not mentioned the move to Phoenix, but he'd become more effusive in his compliments. Clearly he was beginning to take more notice of her accomplishments.

Glancing up at the shelf that ran two feet beneath the high ceiling of the huge office, Ellen surveyed the row of stuffed animals and other bright toys that ringed the room. It was part of what she loved about this place, and this *was* home now, but in Phoenix, she'd have more freedom to live the kind of life that was right for her. She wouldn't have to lie anymore. She'd heard that things were different outside the home office and knew that there she could be her own woman.

With a deep sigh, Ellen felt for the shoes she'd slipped off beneath her desk. She slid her feet into her plain black pumps, placed her briefcase on her desk, turned in her chair and rose—bumping right into the person behind her.

"Pardon me. I'm so sorry," she said immediately, taking a step backward.

"Hey, there's no need for formalities among lovers, Ellen," a low, husky voice whispered. "It's only me. Just Josh."

Half a shriek escaped her mouth before Ellen clamped down on her lips and swallowed the rest.

"Josh!" She turned and looked up over the hand now covering her lips, way up, at the man towering over her. He was smiling, one dark eyebrow raised.

"Oh yes. Now, that's the blue-eyed Ellen I remember. I just don't remember those eyes being quite that wide. Are you that surprised to see me…darling?"

Ellen blinked and furrowed her brow, totally incapable of finding her voice. She carefully slid her hand away from her mouth.

Josh tilted his head, his amber eyes studying her. "Uh-oh, a frown. I guess I *don't* call you darling?" he whispered. "All right. Three guesses. Let's see. Angel?"

Ellen thought she would explode. "You can't be here," she said, as low and fiercely as she could manage without making a scene.

"Oops. Too late, I'm here," he said smoothly. "And I guess I don't call you angel, either, then. *Not* baby," he said, shaking his head. "I'm pretty damn certain I'd never call you 'baby.' You don't look like you'd stand for that. Is it…sweetheart, then?"

He was wearing a wicked grin, one lock of his nearly black hair falling carelessly over his forehead. Ellen had almost forgotten just what a deadly smile Josh Hawthorne possessed. She'd always pretended she hadn't noticed, but then no woman with functioning nerve endings could really ignore the fact that Josh Hawthorne could melt polar ice caps with that smile.

"It's just Ellen," she insisted. "And I promise, if you'll go, I'll explain. Later. If you'll just…leave. Please?" she added, trying for once to make him get serious.

"Leave, Ellen?" Josh asked, taking a step closer. "But why? I understand we're engaged. Don't we want to spend all our time together?"

He had moved two steps closer, forcing her to bend her neck back to talk to him. Dressed in khaki pants, a white shirt that emphasized strong shoulders and a silk tie, he looked like he belonged here. But he didn't. And certainly not this close. He was just being Josh, playing his games, taking his revenge on her for using him. She deserved it, she knew she did, and she'd apologize as soon as she could, but...

"Josh?" she said, her voice quivering slightly as she looked up at him. "Please don't do this. Don't—"

He reached out, brushing a finger softly across her lips.

She closed them immediately, her words stalling in her throat as one of her co-workers passed by, smiling as she noticed Ellen backed up against her desk, half-hidden by the tall man before her.

Josh studied the panicked blue eyes staring up at him. Ellen Rhoades had always been in control, a serious little elf who acted as if work was the most important thing in the world. But those eyes—even nine years ago he'd realized that those huge silver-blue eyes had turned a relatively plain face into something extraordinary.

Maybe it had been those vulnerable, shimmering eyes that had convinced him to come when Penny had told him that Ellen had borrowed his name and was digging her grave. But no, of course not. Not a chance. Nobody in his right mind would leave the bed of a luscious, willing lady and the temptations that Rome could offer for a pair of blue eyes, no matter how wide and intriguing they were. And certainly Josh Hawthorne wouldn't. He didn't commit himself to causes, or to helping ladies in distress. No, like his father before him, his inability to commit was all too often what was *causing* the lady's distress.

Josh resisted the urge to blow out a deep breath and ask himself the question Penny had asked him just ten minutes ago when he'd called her. Why *was* he here? But there was really no point in asking. He knew why he was here. Because the dark-eyed lady had bored him after a few days just as every woman he'd met in the last few years had done. Because Rome wasn't as exciting as it had been in the past, because the business of entertaining and offering legal advice to a few wealthy clients had proven no more satisfying in Europe than it had in the States. He needed a surprise, a challenge in his life, and besides, it was almost too hard to believe that straitlaced Ellen had caught herself up in a risky venture that required some serious acting and an entire bundle of lies. He'd come for the pure entertainment value of this moment, and he was definitely getting his money's worth. The room was practically humming with people whispering, looking their way, doing everything but pointing. Ellen's breathing was speeding up, her eyes sending signals only a totally heartless jerk would fail to pick up on. She was in way over her head and clearly in need of assistance.

He leaned close, placed his lips next to her ear. To an observer, it might even look like he was nuzzling her skin. Josh smiled at the thought.

"Just stay calm," he whispered. "And stop fiddling with the lapels of your jacket. You look nervous."

She placed her hands palms down against his chest and pushed lightly. "I *am* nervous," she whispered back fiercely. "You don't understand—"

He cupped her hands lightly with his own, trapping them against his chest. "Of course I understand," he said, his voice so low it sounded like a caress. "You and I are engaged, and for the past few weeks, I've been the perfect fiancé. I send you presents and I stay out of your life. Just the kind of fiancée I'd want. Not, of course, that I'm looking, mind you. A man is entitled to only one fiancée at a time, I'm pretty sure."

He watched the pale pink rise slowly up her slender throat, suffusing her cheekbones and coloring her hairline. Lovely—but off limits. At least under ordinary circumstances, Ellen was the one woman who'd always seen him for what he was. She'd warned Penny that he'd never play for keeps, and he'd known Ellen as the woman who would never agree to play his games. No, normally, he'd never even get close to her.

Josh trailed one finger from the arch of her brow down to the curve of her jawline. "Darn, Ellen, I didn't know you blushed so prettily. A man really ought to know those things before he marries a woman, don't you think?"

"Josh?" Ellen's fingers clenched more tightly on his shirtfront. He could feel the warmth of her fingertips through the cotton of his shirt.

He tilted his head, waiting for her to finish.

"Please go away," she whispered. "Right now. I have work to do."

Glancing at the briefcase waiting on her desk, Josh tapped his watch and shook his head. "Damn, Ellen, Penny was right. You really do need more practice at lying. You don't look convincing at all. In fact you look darn…irritated."

He leaned around her, his warmth swirling near as he reached over and picked up the box of chocolates on her desk, and held it out. "Stop frowning at me and have a piece of chocolate, sweetheart. It's a mood enhancer. Some people even consider it an aphrodisiac. I'm sure that must be why I sent these to you." Then he squinted, looking at the scribbled message on the box. "All my love, Josh? Damn, I can't remember writing that. You'd think a guy like me would have a better memory, and be a bit more original. I'll just have to be more creative the next time I send you something, won't I?"

"Out," she said between clenched teeth. "Now."

He pulled back, moving his hands to her shoulders and

studying her expression. "Tell me, Ellen, are we having our first fight? I honestly can't remember."

Just then, however, Ellen's hands clamped down on his own, so tightly that he was sure he'd bear the imprint of her small, slender fingers for hours to come. Her wide eyes grew wider still, more frightened. Her breathing kicked up a whole notch. She was clearly upset, and Josh wanted to slap himself for dragging this teasing on so long. Ellen had always been a quiet, nose-to-the-grindstone type, and he'd always teased her about that, but she'd never been in this kind of a risky situation before. He knew from what Penny had told him that Ellen's job meant a lot to her. Just because he didn't completely understand her commitment to a company or what had motivated her to step so far out of character to play this game, didn't mean he didn't admire her. She was one hell of a lady, and she was scared right now. The thought that someone could do that to an innocent like her made Josh's gut clench with anger.

He gave her hands a reassuring squeeze just as a deep, rolling voice sounded behind him.

"Ellen, is this your young man, here at last?"

Her gasp was barely audible, but close as he was, Josh heard it. He felt her fingers tremble beneath his own.

Tarenton, no doubt. Penny had told him about Ellen's boss. Right now he wanted to sock the guy, but that wouldn't do Ellen a bit of good. She wouldn't thank him. Without further thought, Josh turned, thrusting out one hand. "No question. You've got to be the fabled Hugh Tarenton. Ellen's told me so much about you. She's a big fan of yours. Allow me to introduce myself. I'm—"

"That smooth-talking devil who stole our Ellen's heart. Dammit boy, I was beginning to think I'd never get the chance to meet you in person. Ellen didn't mention the fact that you were coming home. I thought you were supposed to be in Italy for several more months.''

''Months?'' Josh said the word on a groan as if Tarenton had just meted out a prison term.

Ellen looked up to see Josh gazing down at her as though she'd suddenly turned into some other person, some wild and beautifully seductive woman. ''Well, it's the truth. I *was* supposed to be in Europe for a while, but,'' he said, sliding his arm around her shoulder, the warm, masculine scent of him filling her senses, ''I'll tell you something, Hugh. I couldn't last that long. There's a limit to how long a man can stay away from the woman who gives him his reason for living.''

God, she hoped her face wasn't flaming. If Mr. Tarenton only knew—Josh had never loved a woman in his life. In the brief time she'd known the man, he'd drifted from one lovely lady to the next. The cavalier son of a known womanizer, Josh's feet had been planted firmly in the family footsteps. He'd probably left a dozen women crying into their hankies back in Italy.

Mr. Tarenton beamed at her and Josh. ''Hell, I like a man who's not afraid to admit that the woman he loves makes him shake just to think of her. Hope we'll be seeing a lot of you now that you're here in town. Lots of company functions coming up. We want you to be a part of the Tarenton family now that you're marrying our Ellen.''

''Well, my first priority is spending some time with Ellen. We've been apart too long,'' Josh said, stroking his hand up and down Ellen's arm. A shiver ripped through her, and she wondered how often he'd used that move and how many other women had trembled in his arms. Angry at herself for even thinking such a thing, she struggled to dredge up a smile.

"I feel like I need to get to know her all over again," Josh continued, smiling down at Ellen.

Mr. Tarenton laughed and pounded Josh on the back. "Well, I can't really blame you for wanting to keep your lady to yourself for a while. But once you've had a chance to settle in, I hope you won't be a stranger. Don't try to keep him to yourself, Ellen," he warned, smiling at her.

"I wouldn't dream of being so selfish, Mr. Tarenton," she said. "Believe me, I wouldn't."

"Besides, I'm hoping Ellen will give me a tour of this place when she gets a chance. This looks like a great company to build a career," Josh said, motioning to the life-size set of building blocks displayed over by the watercooler.

"Damn, I like the choice you've made," Tarenton repeated, turning to Ellen. "Have I told you that? This man is going to fit right into our way of life."

This man is going to be gone as soon as the wind blows in another direction, Ellen thought as Josh and Mr. Tarenton shook hands once again and her boss said his farewells before walking away. Josh Hawthorne was not real. He was the man in the picture, a man you could make up stories about, a man you could call a pretend fiancé, but Josh in the flesh was a fleeting thing, a dangerous article.

As the room emptied, Josh turned to her. He smiled that devastating smile, and Ellen found she couldn't look away. She knew darn well why Mr. Tarenton had been so impressed. It was impossible to look at this man and not dream unrealistic dreams.

"You frown too much, Ellen," he said. "Way too much." And brushing his fingers lightly up between her eyes, he smoothed out the lines there that furrowed her brow. Of their own accord, her lids drifted shut as she felt the pads of his fingers stroke her skin.

Warm lips brushed against her own, sending golden currents of feeling coursing through her body.

Ellen opened her eyes, and stepped back. "What was that about?" But she knew. Of course, she knew. He'd been laughing at her ever since he walked into the room. She'd been using him, shamelessly using him. Now he was just getting back some of his own, making her pay for her duplicity.

Josh folded her hand in his own. He started toward the door through the near-empty office. "It was just a kiss, Ellen. If we're engaged, we *do* kiss, don't we?"

She should be mad. He was teasing her again, trying to punish her. But he had saved her butt back there when Mr. Tarenton had stepped in. He had charmed the man the way he'd always charmed everyone, especially women.

"I'm so sorry," she said, stopping dead in her tracks and turning to him. "I really am."

"For what?"

For tons of things she could think of right now. For putting him in this position, for using his name without asking. Mostly though, Ellen realized, staring up into those jewel-like amber eyes, watching those thick masculine lashes, she was sorry that she had chosen Josh Hawthorne as the man to build her story around. A fictional character would have been less convincing, but he would have been easier. A fictional character would never have shown up and shaken her world. A made-up man wouldn't be making her quiver right now with the desire to be kissed one more time.

Oh hell, she thought, closing her eyes to Josh Hawthorne and his damned infuriating sex appeal. She was going to have to jilt her fiancé and start again. That was all there was to it. She only hoped Mr. Tarenton would understand.

Chapter Two

Ellen bumped against Josh as they neared her car in the Tarenton Toys parking lot.

"I—I *am* sorry," she said, stopping in her tracks, turning to face him. She held her head high, knowing that she had earned his anger.

He started to shake his head in dismissal, but she reached out and touched his arm. "I mean that I'm sorry for stealing your name," she clarified. "I really had no right to do that."

Josh stopped beside her tidy little subcompact, resting one large hand on the roof. His long, lean frame made Ellen feel small, and when she looked up at him, all traces of humor had faded from those amber shards that targeted her. The wind lifted dark strands of his hair, emphasizing the rough planes of his face, usually masked by a smile.

"Why *did* you? Choose me, I mean?" he asked, cutting away all the polite rhetoric and going straight to the heart of the matter.

But that was a question Ellen wasn't sure she wanted to answer, not when she wasn't completely sure she understood her reasoning in the first place. Oh, there were the reasons she'd given herself. She did, after all, have all those convenient pictures. But it wasn't as if she really knew Josh well. Although he and Penny still talked on the phone frequently, they'd only dated for three months, and her own contact with him during that time had been predominantly limited to Josh's teasing that she never took her nose out of a textbook long enough to even mumble "hello." That and the fact that she had discouraged Penny from dating him.

"I'm—not sure," she said as Josh continued to stare down at her. "Penny had mentioned that you were wandering around Europe and it seemed as if you would be...safe."

What a joke. As if Josh had ever seemed safe. He'd broken more hearts than she'd broken fingernails, and given the fact that the only things he was committed to were bachelorhood and the pursuit of entertainment, he was the last man she should have chosen. He was not marriage material, and anyone who'd ever met him would realize that. But then, no one at Tarenton had ever met Josh—until now. He *had* seemed safe.

"I apologize completely for doing something so despicable, and I will, of course, take care of things immediately. You don't have to worry about me bandying your name about anymore." She curled her fingers into nervous fists.

Josh reached out, caught one of her hands in his, stroking her knuckles gently until her fingers unfurled. "And how will you take care of things this time, Ellen?" he coaxed gently.

She tried to ignore the feathery sensation of Josh's

touch. "I'll explain that once we'd seen each other again, we realized we weren't right for each other."

"Even though your supervisor seemed to approve of the match. And even though getting rid of me will put you back to square one. Maybe even harm your cause?"

Ellen closed her eyes. "Josh, what exactly did Penny tell you? And why? I can't believe she betrayed me that way."

She could feel Josh bending closer, and she opened startled eyes.

"We're being observed," he explained, nodding to the upper offices of the building. "And as for Penny, well, don't blame her. She knows you don't want to get married, and she was worried that you'd gotten in over your head. She felt responsible for giving you my photo, and she thought maybe I'd be interested in helping. I am, you know."

"You're really not angry, then? You should be. *I* would be."

Josh grinned and arched one wicked ebony brow. "I'm sure you would be, but then, you and I were never very much alike, were we? I'm not angry. In fact, I can see how a woman who plays by the rules the way you do got yourself pushed into this corner. Easily. We're talking about discrimination here, Ellen. That's what's happening and you know it. Penny says you've proven yourself and earned your stripes five times over but that Hugh Tarenton is holding them ransom until you buy into the company line. And while you could become a whistle-blower—well, who doesn't know that such methods often backfire? I don't blame you for becoming a bit creative given the situation. It's just…Ellen Rhoades becoming an actress?" Josh held out his hands in disbelief.

Ellen managed a genuine smile then. "I know. I feel

as if I've grown an extra nose or two in the past few weeks. I'm not really very good at playing a part, but then I haven't done all that much. Not really. Just the pictures and a few gifts..." She trailed off.

Josh crossed his arms. "Still apologizing, Ellen? Don't. Let's agree that you're in a crazy, unfair position and that I'm here to help you. Hell, Ellen, I've always enjoyed a good game. You know that, and frankly, you've done me a favor. I was getting a little tired of Europe when I got that letter from Penny. I was in the mood for a little righteous indignation and a new adventure."

"And I'm the new adventure?"

Josh brushed one finger lightly across her nose. His smile was gentle. "Sweetheart, I don't want to see anyone push you around. You get married when you're good and ready and not before. It's a wonderful institution, I'm sure, but definitely not meant for everyone."

His words, which so closely echoed her own of a few days before, struck a painful chord in Ellen's heart. There was a time when she'd once had dreams like all little girls, but she'd learned the truth of Josh's words. Some people just weren't made for marriage. Two of them were standing in the parking lot of Tarenton Toys right now. How ironic that the world believed those same two people were the perfect couple.

"Some people would say this is just a job..." she began uncertainly. "I myself feel horribly guilty lying at all."

Josh took her chin between his thumb and forefinger. She knew that there were people watching, that he was playing the game he'd come to play. "That's because you have a conscience, Ellen. And while I'm sure it's a good thing for some people to have, yours, I'm afraid, is working overtime in this case. Nobody who'd ever met you, lady, could fail to realize that you dedicate yourself completely to whatever venture you undertake. If you've worked and put your all into this place, then we're not talking about something that's just a job, Ellen. Even I know that you're a lady who would give more than one hundred percent of yourself to any endeavor you decided to undertake. If this is important to you, don't feel guilty. Just think about what the next step will be.''

Her mind drew a blank. She'd always hoped that simply making Mr. Tarenton believe she was engaged would be enough. If that didn't work, what more could she do?

Josh stared down into Ellen's eyes, which mirrored her confusion. He felt a fierce shaft of anger lance through him. Maybe he didn't have much personal experience with commitment. The son of ''love 'em and leave 'em Les Hawthorne,'' Josh knew he was his father's son in all the most vital ways. He'd always had a guilt-inspiring urge to leave every woman he'd ever known, he'd never experienced the kind of love and loyalty that made a real marriage…the only kind he wanted. Devotion, he'd learned, just wasn't a word in his vocabulary.

But this lady standing before him wasn't like that. Not at all. When she dedicated herself to something she went at it heart and soul. The thought that she had given her all to this company only to have someone try to force marriage down her throat made Josh's temperature rise. She was a grown woman, an intelligent lady, but she was as lost as a newborn babe in these waters. Josh knew all about manipulative people like Tarenton. He'd learned from his father, a man who could sell ice in Antarctica as easily as he could convince himself he loved a woman enough for marriage when he only wanted her bed for a while. Les had just taken wife number five. So Josh knew that there were people who could smile and cause heart-ache in the same second. He recognized the species when he saw it.

"Sweetheart, that man's raised this company from the ground up. He knows how to get what he wants. If you want to beat him at his game, you've got to really make him believe you're panting to get married. You're going to have to wade in with your eyes closed and let the water rush over your head. But don't worry. You'll be standing on my shoulders. I won't let you drown."

"This doesn't sound like much fun for you," she said, biting her lip. "What are you going to get out of this whole scenario?"

He raised one eyebrow wickedly. "A challenge."

"A game?"

"The best kind," he admitted. "One where the stakes are high, and the payoff is seeing justice done."

"Maybe you should have just made a career out of the courtroom," she suggested, looking up at him skeptically.

"Aw, Ellen, you wound me. Is that a reprimand about what I've chosen to do with my law degree?"

She shook her head. "I don't tell people how to run their lives, Josh."

He laughed out loud then, turning her around and taking her hand. "Maybe not," he agreed. "But your eyes speak volumes, Ellen. And right now they're telling me that you heartily disapprove of the fact that I spend my time counseling the rich and famous."

She shrugged. "Obviously those people need your help, or they wouldn't pay you for your assistance. Josh, my car's back there," she said, stopping in her tracks as he led her away from the spot where her subcompact was parked,

"Exactly," he said. "And you and I are an engaged couple who haven't seen each other in months. Everyone knows that I'm counting the seconds till I can slip you out of that fussy little suit and into my bed. There's no way, Ellen, that we're going to waste this opportunity by driving away in separate cars. With the world watching," he added, giving a slight nod toward the windows of the office, "you and I are going to climb into my car and drive directly to my hotel."

Josh felt Ellen's step falter slightly as he slid his hand beneath the jacket of her suit, resting his palm on her waist. The silk of her blouse slipped beneath his fingers, revealing the warmth of her skin through the thin material. She was uncertain, he could tell, but no more than he was. He wanted to help her, it was true, but he wished that Ellen had been less appealing, that her eyes had been duller, her skin less smooth and soft. With every step, her flesh brushed against the nerve endings in the tips of his fingers.

She laughed nervously. "You must think I'm very inexperienced and stupid. I'm not very good at this sort of thing," she began.

Hell, inexperienced and stupid were the last adjectives in the world he would apply to her right now. Innocent. Exciting. Alluring as hell. Yes, all of those. He felt like a heel just for touching her. He was getting way too much enjoyment out of this.

Clearing his throat and clamping down on the tightening in his groin, Josh looked at Ellen. "You don't have to be good at this, Ellen. Just follow my lead and when we're in public try to think of me as the man you're dying to marry. Don't be afraid that I'll take anything personally. Think of this as just another job you're doing, if it helps. No one is ever going to know that when we get back to my room, all we're going to do is grab some food and plot our strategy. When I drive you home, your neighbors will see you're coming home late. They aren't going to know if you were rolling in the hay or playing gin rummy. Just remember that. People will believe what they want to believe, and if our public behavior leads them to think that things are going on in private that are never really going to happen, that's good. That's convincing.''

As Josh handed her into his car and climbed in on the driver's side, he turned to see Ellen staring at him, one corner of her mouth quirked up.

"You really should have gone into litigation," she told him. "I don't think a jury would have stood a chance around you."

"Nah," he said, shaking his head. "A court of law's got too many rules. Even with all my wealth, I'd be penniless by now, fined into poverty for contempt of court.''

"Maybe," she agreed, settling down in her seat. "But I'm not so sure. At any rate, I'm glad you're here and not in some courtroom, Josh. Thank you for coming to my rescue. I just hope I can be as convincing as you are.''

"Don't worry," he assured her. "By the end of next week, everyone will be laying bets on what kind of wallpaper we'll be hanging in our nursery. We're going to be the perfect couple. Satisfaction guaranteed.''

Except he was not going to be truly satisfied, Josh realized, checking to make sure the lady beside him was wearing her seat belt and finding, that, of course, she was. He hadn't forgotten that Ellen always followed all the rules. But it seemed he'd forgotten how damned seductive those big baby blues of hers were. She made a man want to touch her, slide his hands beneath those man-tailored business suits and peel away the layers to the silky feminine skin beneath.

Josh nearly groaned in frustration. He'd touched plenty of women in his time and he'd left many holding out their hands hungrily. But this time he was going to be the one with the hungry hands. Because there was no way in hell he could allow himself to touch Ellen Rhoades. She was not like the other women he spent his time with; he'd always known that. She had never elected to play the game—and he was damn well not going to introduce her to it. He would ignore those lustful urges she called up in him, would place his hands and lips on her only in public when both of them would be "on-stage" and unaffected; he'd never allow himself more than that—even if he had to dredge up old legal history and recite a monotonous litany of court cases to distract himself. No matter what his body said, Josh intended to leave Ellen right where she wanted to be, on the fast track to her career, unscathed, unattached and smiling when he walked away. It was the one commitment he was willing to make.

"Are you sure we need to do all this?" Ellen was curled up on a plush chair in Josh's hotel room, her legs tucked half beneath her as she scribbled furiously on a yellow legal pad. She tugged her navy skirt down with her left hand as she continued to list Josh's suggestions with her right. "Josh!" she said suddenly, scratching out what she'd just copied. "We are not going to a travel agent to plan an exotic vacation on some obscure Caribbean Island. Things are never going to get that far."

Josh walked over to the chair where she was seated. Gently he removed the pad of paper from her grasp.

"Do you have to write everything down, sweetheart?"

Ellen glanced up suddenly at the endearment. She looked toward the door, wondering if Josh had heard someone on the other side. But no, that was probably just Josh. He was the kind of man who loved women, all women, in a very broadminded kind of way. Endearments fell from his lips without conscious thought or meaning.

"I'll forget something if I don't make a list," she reasoned, finally answering his question as he continued to stand there. "It's the way I always do things, the way I work. How else would I manage to stay on top of all the things I'm in charge of?"

He squatted beside her chair, looking up at her. "And it's a very good way of doing things under normal circumstances," he soothed. "But, Ellen, we're not planning a trip to the grocery store together. We're supposed to be a man and a woman lost in the throes of love and passion. We're discussing our plans now so that we're in agreement later, but you don't want it to look like you're going at this in a mechanical fashion. To the world at large, we're following our hearts, not a list. And yes, I do think we need to do all this. It would look a bit odd if we didn't plan a honeymoon, don't you think?"

She tucked her bare toes a bit farther beneath her and let out a sigh. "All right, a honeymoon, but not an island. I can't afford that kind of vacation, Josh."

His laugh was low and husky. He had discarded his tie, rolled up his sleeves to reveal tanned and muscled forearms. If anyone had entered the room, they might well have thought there was more going on here than there was, Ellen reasoned. But of course, she knew better.

"We're just planning, Ellen, not spending. But if it came to that, I can afford the cost."

Ellen sat up straight in her chair, sliding her feet to the plush blue carpeting. "Absolutely not. This is my problem. You're not to spend any money, even if you are as rich as the Rockefellers. Do you understand, Josh Hawthorne?''

As he rose to his feet and raised his hands in mock surrender, Ellen noticed that his eyes were still crinkled in amusement.

''And if it came down to actually having to spend money,'' she continued, ''I...I don't think I'd want to waste it on the Caribbean. That's not my way.''

Josh studied the legal pad as if the answers to some great mystery were written there. ''And what is your way, Ellen? If you had the time and means to go anywhere you wanted to, where exactly would you go?''

She stared back at him, her brow furrowed in concentration.

''Where do you usually go on your vacations?'' he prompted gently.

Biting her lip, Ellen wished she'd left this subject alone. ''I...I've been pretty busy these past few years.''

Josh flung the legal pad to the bed. He crossed his arms. ''Are you telling me that you haven't taken a vacation lately?''

She raised her chin. ''I visited my brother in Boise two Christmases ago,'' she said defiantly. ''That counts.''

Josh looked like he was fighting not to smile. ''And you expect a man to take his bride to Boise on a honeymoon, Ellen?''

The hot color was tracing its way up her throat. She just knew it was. ''No,'' she said quietly. ''Of course not, but...''

''So where would you go, Ellen Rhoades,'' he challenged. ''If you could go anywhere you wanted, if we found ourselves pushed into a corner and we ended up actually going down to the wire on this engagement, where would we tell people we were going on our honeymoon? Isn't there anywhere you've always wanted to go but never allowed yourself to see?''

Closing her eyes, Ellen let Josh's seductive voice drift over her. She was a practical woman, it had been years since she'd dreamed the kind of dreams Josh was challenging her to dredge up, but somewhere, some while ago...

''I—I've always wanted to go to Maine,'' she admitted hesitantly, blinking her eyes, hoping he wouldn't laugh at her foolishness.

''A cottage on the beach?'' he suggested.

She smiled as she realized he was not going to make a joke out of her comment. ''Yes,'' she answered quietly.

''Then that's our honeymoon,'' he agreed in a voice like a whisper. ''Someplace where the wind can slip through your hair and you can forget about work for a while. You won't even have to wear shoes for the entire time,'' he said, grinning down to where she'd once again discarded her pumps.

She glanced down at her toes outlined in silk. She'd always had this terrible habit of shucking her shoes as soon as she entered the house. Maybe because when her parents left her in charge of four children, she'd always been the one who needed to make sure that no one wore out their shoes too soon. Silly, but now with Josh examining her nearly bare feet, she felt...exposed. Naked. Silly.

''I think it would be all right if I go home now,'' she said suddenly, swallowing as she quickly put her shoes on. ''If anyone was paying attention to us, they're gone already. And I have to work tomorrow.''

Josh nodded, fishing his keys out of his pocket. ''I'll take you back to retrieve your car. And Ellen?''

She looked up from where she was repacking her brief-case, stashing her pad of paper inside.

"Don't worry. In spite of all those lists, we're not going to take this to extremes," he assured her. "I don't think Tarenton's going to want to see the signed marriage certificate. He'll probably cave quickly once he's sure you're stepping into line. We'll just take things slowly at first."

Nodding, she joined him as he held the door for her.

Thirty minutes later, he pulled up behind her at her door.

"You really didn't have to follow me," she insisted, as he waited for her to find her keys and insert them in the lock of her apartment.

"Lady, it's two in the morning. There are wolves on the prowl, and I'm not talking about myself."

Ellen gazed up at him, biting her lip. "Don't insult yourself, Josh. I know you and I have been at odds at times. I did, after all, warn Penny away from you. But I appreciate the fact that you're helping me now…for whatever reasons. I wouldn't accuse you of anything like that."

He shrugged, studying her as she reached behind her and turned the knob. There was an uncomfortable moment of silence as they stared at each other.

"I—I don't think we have to worry about anyone seeing us right now," she whispered, hoping he didn't feel obligated to kiss her for the benefit of her neighbors.

"Probably not," he agreed in a low voice, not backing away. "But just in case—"

He reached out, gently grasping her hand, lifting it as he studied her ringless fingers nesting in his. Turning her palm to his view, he touched his lips to the naked flesh. Once. Twice. Her skin burned, then went suddenly cold when he dragged his mouth away. The need to look down to where their hands still joined them—surely that searing contact had left a mark—was nearly overwhelming. Steeling herself, she resisted the urge.

''I'll see you tomorrow, Ellen,'' he promised, relinquishing her hand and opening the door for her.

As she stepped inside and dropped her head back against the closed door, she listened to the muffled sound of his retreat. She heard and felt the battering of her heart against her chest…and she knew what she had always known.

Josh Hawthorne was just too much for a woman like her to handle. If she were honest, she'd admit that *no* female on earth had ever been able to handle him, least of all her. She could deal with corporate demands, soothe irate employees, organize and oversee meetings and training programs at a moment's notice without even blinking, but the truth was that she was not all that experienced in the kind of relationships Josh excelled in. What's more, she didn't even want a man in her life. She was sure of that. It was just that this particular man was so much larger than life, so dizzying, so overwhelmingly…Josh. He made her feel things she didn't want to feel.

Thank goodness he had a plan that would send them spinning away from each other soon. Once she was in Arizona she'd never have to see him again. She should look forward to that. She really should.

Chapter Three

When Josh entered the hallowed halls of Tarenton Toys the next day, Ellen was standing in the middle of the office. She had a file under one arm, a telephone receiver under the other and a long line of people waiting to see her.

He watched as she held up one hand and spoke into the receiver briefly, cocking her head to one side as another employee needing her attention arrived. Two minutes later, she concluded her conversation, hung up the phone and automatically turned to the first man waiting in line. The smile she produced was pure Ellen, utterly gentle and sincere.

"Mr. Fredericks, I'm sorry, but this prototype is still just not exactly what we had in mind. Here's a list of the changes Mr. Tarenton would like to see. But please don't worry," she soothed to the man who was obviously agitated. "I don't have a single doubt this is going to be your best invention yet. You have a way with toys that has always amazed me, and by the looks of your fan mail,

I'm not alone. I just got through reading a stack of letters from children all over the country, almost all about your creations, so…please don't get discouraged. The kids are all counting on you. I know you'll be able to work through this to everyone's satisfaction. It *is* a wonderful idea.''

The man opened his mouth, then closed it again. He held out his hands, then finally shrugged and smiled sheepishly, before heading purposefully toward a door in the back of the room, taking his invention with him.

The phone began to ring again.

As Josh watched, Ellen moved smoothly from one crisis to the next. He wondered if things backed up like this often. She'd obviously become skilled at handling high-pressure situations. It occurred to him that she might not really need his help—but then there *was* Penny's letter, and all that it implied. Ellen, he could see, was one very qualified employee. She was also, however, a lady who played by the rules. And this time the rules had been thrown out the door—or maybe in her face.

She needed him.

The thought warmed him, made him want to wrap the strength of his arms around her and protect her from all the Hugh Tarentons of the world. He wasn't sure why, but he knew one thing. It would be pure foolishness to place much credence on his feelings, no matter how warm. They'd pass in time. He'd learned to wait them out, because unlike his father, he didn't offer lies—to himself or anyone. He might have disappointed women by his inability to care, but at least he hadn't ever offered empty, damaging hope and promises to any woman. Nor had he ever fathered a child who'd have to learn to deal with his lack of commitment.

Josh blacked out the pointless thought and the memories it dredged up. Tossing all sense of self aside, he zeroed in on Ellen as soon as the throngs had disbanded.

"So, is this the eye of the storm, or do you have more than two minutes to yourself?" he asked, placing his hands on her shoulders as she sat at her desk. "Speak softly, sweetheart," he urged as she gasped. "We want people to wonder what we're saying even if we're saying nothing. I'm supposed to know you intimately, remember? So tell me...about your job, your day."

The muscles that framed Ellen's delicate shoulders tensed beneath his fingertips as she tilted her head up, trying to see him.

"Oh, it's actually pretty slow around here today," she finally said, her voice a quiet thrum flowing through her body and into his own. "At least no one's sick or on vacation. By the way, I wanted to thank you...I think." She motioned toward the miniature stuffed koala sitting on her desk. "I wasn't sure..."

"A bit juvenile?" Josh asked, bending low over her shoulder to whisper near her ear. "But it *is* a Tarenton product. Didn't your boss notice?"

Ellen's hair brushed against his jaw and Josh breathed in cinnamon...apples. Only he'd never associated such homey scents with blue eyes, the naked curve of a shoulder and tangled sheets before. He did now.

She pulled back far enough to look him in the eye. "He did," she said, her voice a soft trace of sound meant for his ears only. "Of course, he did. He was beaming, ecstatic. That was so thoughtful of you, but..." She reached out, tracing the lettering on the card that dangled from the sweet little creature's neck. Her cheeks were delightfully suffused with color.

Josh couldn't help tilting up the corner of his lips. He reached out, touching the card she held.

"Sweetheart, I'll never forget the way you looked last night with your hair flowing gently over your shoulders," he quoted, without opening the card. "Blue eyes, beauty, soft skin, sweetness. I don't know how I'll ever last until tonight. Josh."

Ellen nervously licked her lips, she took a deep breath. She was clutching the edge of her desk, her knuckles white.

"Ellen, have you been blushing like that all day?" he whispered.

Her blue eyes flew open wide. She sucked in air. "It's just that—I don't get cards like this every day," she explained, crossing her arms, and her legs. "Mr. Tarenton read the card, then he started smiling. He's been smiling all day. Heaven only knows what the man is thinking."

"That he'd like to go home at lunch and make love to Mrs. Tarenton?" Josh suggested, trying not to laugh as he settled himself on the edge of her desk.

"Don't mock me, Josh. I'm not good at this sort of thing. Ask me to conduct seminars or handle a disgruntled employee or how to fit twelve hours of work into ten hours. I can do all those things, but I don't know what to say when I know that people are looking at me and imagining me having torrid sex with a man."

"*Making love* to the man you're marrying," Josh amended, tucking one finger under her chin and forcing her to look into his eyes. "That's what they think was happening, Ellen. Remember? That's why we're doing this. And as for your Mr. Tarenton—"

"Yes?"

"Next time, sweetheart," Josh whispered, a bare six inches from her luscious mouth, his fingers resting beneath her chin. "Try telling him that those words were meant for your eyes alone. That was a message from the man who loves you, and it wasn't meant for public consumption. I should be able to send you gifts and leave the card blank or even write the words to 'Mary Had a Little Lamb' without anyone being the wiser.''

"You think I should reprimand Mr. Tarenton? You think that would work?'' Josh could feel Ellen swallowing, the muscles in her neck contracting beneath the velvet of her skin.

"I think,'' he said, trying to ignore the feel of her, "that any man who thinks he can dictate his employees' lives isn't likely to pay much attention to the rules of society. That's why I wrote that card. Because I was pretty damn sure he would read it, and I wanted him to know how things were between us. But still,'' he said, sitting back and smiling at her, "you might consider reminding him that there are such rules, anyway. It's clear that you're a valuable employee. I doubt he'd fire you for trying to maintain a small shred of your privacy. You might think about it. Over lunch with me. Would you do me the honor? I've got something we need to talk about.''

Ellen returned his smile. "Of course, and thank you. For not thinking I was acting silly.'' But as she rose to leave her desk, Ellen turned back, reaching for a drawer. "I nearly forgot. These are for you.''

There was still a slight glow to her skin, but she was smiling up at him expectantly as she held out a small container of cookies, obviously homemade. "I remembered that you were always a sucker for chocolate macadamia cookies. It's just a small token. They're not as good as the ones Penny and I used to get from the bakery,'' she said with a shrug as they exited the office. "Not much, but somehow I thought you ought to be getting more out of this than the thrill of a challenge,'' she admitted.

For the first time in a long time, Josh was left speechless. She'd baked him cookies. Late last night or early this morning—when else had she had time? His throat felt suddenly gritty and tight. Not that he'd never had a gift from a woman before. There'd been many. Women had bought him extravagant offerings, set up seduction scenes, but the ladies he hung with always wanted something they were afraid he couldn't give. Not this lady. She already had all he had to offer and all she wanted. Yet she'd noted and remembered something he'd nearly forgotten himself, that he'd been wont to filch cookies from her cookie jar. It was stupid, it was crazy, but Ellen had once again managed to catch him off guard and affect him in a way he'd never expected.

But of course, she was feeling off-kilter herself, somehow beholden to him, and he didn't want that. Not at all. He just wanted—hell, what he wanted had nothing to do with anything, because what he wanted was to touch her. Slowly. Repeatedly. Rhythmically. Without the shield of clothing separating her nakedness from his. He'd felt that way from the moment he'd walked in the door yesterday and looked in her eyes, but he'd already decided that that was just too bad. He was a grown man, not a kid. He could damn well be an adult and ignore his desires.

What he couldn't ignore was the fact that Ellen seemed to feel his slightest action deserved an answering reaction, a payback, and that rankled, twisted something deep inside him. Hell, he'd explained that his reasons for dropping in on her were totally self-serving. She didn't owe him a thing, and he fully intended to tell her so in no uncertain terms.

So why did he think he was going to have an argument

on his hands as soon as Ellen realized what this lunch was all about?

If she opened those sweet blue eyes wide and tried to thank him again he didn't know what he'd do. A man could only do so much with a woman like Ellen before his lips and his hands got out of line.

Ellen stared across the table at the small box Josh held in his hand. Her fork hung poised in midair.

"You're not wearing an engagement ring, Ellen," he said, matter-of-factly, taking her fork from her and placing it on her plate.

She took a deep breath. "You were out of town," she said, repeating the story she'd fabricated. "We became engaged long-distance. There was no chance to get a ring."

He tilted his head in acquiescence. "Yes, but I'm back now," he reminded her. "It would be a bit too strange if we didn't abide by the formalities." He popped open the black velvet box to reveal an exquisite teardrop-shaped diamond ring.

Ellen planted both palms on the edge of the table, purposefully. She stared Josh dead in the eyes. "It's absolutely lovely, but I'm sure you know...I can't take that."

"Of course you can. Come on, Ellen, don't get cold feet now. We're getting there."

"Josh," she whispered fiercely. "I cannot afford something like that on my salary. And if you say what I think you're going to say—"

"Which is only the truth. *I* can afford this rock. Easily. It's no big deal."

"It's a diamond engagement ring, Josh. Can you take it back? What does a man do with an expensive engagement ring when he's done with it? Someday you'll want to marry. Are you going to give your bride-to-be a slightly used ring?''

Ellen was breathing more heavily now, growing more agitated as Josh's smile grew.

"Now, Ellen, you don't have to worry. I have no plans to get married, so there isn't any poor defenseless woman out there who's going to have to put up with me trying to push a used diamond on her.''

"Then what are you going to do with it? You'll be stuck.''

Josh looked at her speculatively, his long lashes partially concealing his narrowed eyes. "I was thinking you might like to keep it—as a souvenir.''

"No. I couldn't do that. I wouldn't want to do that,'' she said with conviction. When all this was over, she didn't want any reminders of this time. That ring was an expensive prop, too expensive, and Josh was lending it to her because it was part of the game. But also, there was the other impediment, the fact that she was proving to be far too susceptible to this charade and Josh's smile. His heated glances made her shiver—but they weren't real. She needed to keep reminding herself of that.

Because the fact was that Josh and this stage they'd created was a fantasy, an enticing illusion made of smoke. And Ellen knew firsthand what happened to people who tried to make their daydreams come to life—and failed. The price was high. The payment could go on forever. She wasn't going to follow in her parents' and sister's footsteps. When this brief interlude played itself out, she would do her best to put this whole incident behind her. Because she wanted no lingering memories of Josh haunting her and making her wonder what it would have been like to live the fantasy. Not a single one.

"Josh," Ellen said softly. "I can't tell you how much it means to have you in my corner, and I really do thank you for offering, but I just couldn't keep that ring. It would trouble me if I accepted something so costly," she repeated, hoping that Josh would accept that as her reason without digging any deeper.

He smiled slightly, nodding his agreement. "I thought as much. All right then, don't worry. *I'll* keep it to remind me of your success. Now finish eating your lunch, Ellen," he said quietly, taking her hand and slowly slipping the ring on her finger. For two seconds, possibly three, her left hand rested on his palm, before she pulled away. The delicate gold band felt heavy, almost leaden. A lie. This was the kind of treasure Josh should be giving to the woman he loved.

But when she looked up again, he was grinning at her in that boyish way that always made her feel as if she was falling from a great height.

"You sure you don't want lunch, Ellen? I was hoping you would, so I wouldn't feel guilty about having a piece of that double fudge cake they serve here. It's no fun eating chocolate cake alone. Join me?"

She laughed. "All right. But first I have to eat my vegetables, is that it?"

"Something like that," he agreed. "I don't want you getting sick because you're not eating right."

Ellen crossed her arms and tried to look down her nose. "You know perfectly well that I always ate healthy. *You're* the one eating cookies and chocolate cake."

Her laughter bubbled forth like soothing music. Josh leaned back, finally relaxing. She'd been feeling stressed just a moment ago. Deception, he knew, just wasn't her way, and the ring had been tangible proof of their lie, one that had troubled her. Her ensuing laughter reassured him that she was accepting her fate reluctantly, but with grace and good humor, and it was a rare gift, he suspected. Because after watching her this afternoon, Josh understood that the years hadn't changed Ellen all that much. She was still a workaholic and almost totally clueless when it came to kicking up her heels.

"You should laugh more, Ellen. Your face lights up like a lovely, glowing candle."

She stopped laughing then, but her smile lingered. "Josh, you really *are* enjoying this, aren't you. I've been worried. I don't like using people."

"Sweetheart," he said, leaning forward. "Don't worry. Not a bit. This is…most rewarding." And he was forced to admit that it was the truth. In spite of his concerns and the tension of keeping the reins on his libido, he was enjoying this pretense. He couldn't wait for Tarenton to cave in and hand Ellen her promotion on a platter. There was something infinitely…satisfying about pursuing justice. There was something even more satisfying about knowing he had wrung a smile from a woman who had never had much time for smiles. It occurred to Josh that he had a rare opportunity here. He had Ellen Rhoades at his mercy, he had the chance to give her many opportunities to smile and to relax in spite of herself. Damn, if he didn't mean to take advantage of the situation.

Shaking her head, Ellen stared into her coffee cup, but her lips were still tilting slightly at the corners. She waited until Josh had ordered chocolate cake for both of them before she looked up.

"I've never seen anyone get so ecstatic over chocolate cake before," she confided.

Josh shrugged and smiled. "But then, you haven't

tasted this chocolate cake,'' he whispered. ''It's almost an orgasmic experience.''

Ellen sat up straighter. She straightened the already straight lapels on her jacket, brushed back her hair, taking a long, deep breath. ''That good? Well then, maybe I should—''

''Trust me, sweetheart,'' Josh said. ''Just trust me.''

''I do,'' she agreed. And he knew that neither of them was talking about chocolate cake. ''But, Josh, I wish you wouldn't call me sweetheart. Not when we're completely alone. I'd rather you didn't.''

''Agreed. If you'll agree to stop worrying about money or whether I know what I'm doing when I decide to move in on a woman and make her mine.''

A delicate, beautiful pink glow suffused Ellen's cheeks. ''I guess I was being silly earlier. I doubt there are too many men who know more about women and romance than you do,'' she conceded.

She was right. It was true. But somehow hearing the verdict come from Ellen's lips sounded somewhat obscene. Suddenly Josh wished there hadn't been so many women in his life—but then, he was what he was. And so was she.

Still, they'd overcome a barrier here. From now on, Ellen would stop feeling so beholden—he hoped. And he would be free to treat her like the woman he was engaged to, even if that would never be true. He was at liberty to show Ellen the lighter side of life.

Everything was looking good.

Ellen entered the office in front of Josh, feeling a bit more relaxed than she'd felt in the past twenty-four hours. Her guilty conscience had receded a bit. She remembered that Penny had always told her Josh lived to be entertained. If she was, then, the current entertainment, if her situation was providing him with some measure of amusement, that at least soothed her worry about having drawn him away from his own life. She reminded herself that Josh had never done anything he didn't want to and was glad that he wanted to be here—for however long it lasted. By the time he was gone, she would be well on her way to making her move to Phoenix and he'd be moving on to the next show.

A nibble of doubt assailed her, but Ellen pushed away her concern that Josh wasn't as happy as he appeared. Years of raising her siblings had turned her into a bit of a worrier—a trait she fought on a daily basis now that her sister and three brothers were grown. But Josh was an adult, no question of that. He knew his own mind. No way did he need her looking out for him. One had only to look at him to see that. The man exuded confidence from every pore. He was a prime example of a bold, secure male—and he knew it. How absolutely ridiculous for her to even consider the fact that he might need something from her. It was just that "caretaker of the world" gene she owned acting up. No more than that.

Looking back at Josh, Ellen smiled. She'd stepped into this deception out of a sense of frustration and desperation, but for the first time she truly believed that it would work.

Josh's answering smile nearly stole her breath, but that was okay. That was just her usual silly reaction to the man, the way all women reacted to him. Everything was finally falling into place. Everything would be fine in a short time.

"Damn, but you two look good together."

Hugh Tarenton met Ellen and Josh halfway to her desk. He was wearing that same smug look that he always wore when he came up with a new way to push his product or expand his business. Ellen had seen it a thousand times. It usually meant good news for his employees since Mr. Tarenton was at his most magnanimous during these stages. He was prone to give out raises, okay vacations that occurred at inconvenient times and hire less than experienced but enthusiastic neophyte recruits for positions he had previously considered unnecessary.

The fact that he was smiling at her in that way could only mean something positive. Ellen's spirits rose. She reached out and clasped Josh's hand. He deserved to be in on this. After all, it had been his appearance that had pushed things over the edge.

"Thank you, Mr. Tarenton," she answered, unable to contain her own smile. Everything was going to be better than good, she surmised. It was going to be wonderful.

"You two come on in my office," Mr. Tarenton invited. "I've got something we need to talk about. Of course, it's Ellen's decision in the end, but…"

"I'd appreciate the chance to share anything that concerns Ellen," Josh said, his voice so deep and low and close that Ellen felt herself shiver involuntarily. She was glad that Josh was holding her hand tightly. Otherwise she might fall, the relief was so great.

He placed one arm around her waist as he entered the CEO's expansive office and closed the door behind them.

Tarenton was pacing around the room like an excited puppy. He barely waited for them to sit down before he spoke.

"It's been a long time since someone who's been as involved in the company as you have has gotten married, Ellen," he began. "I know that the two of you haven't had much of a chance to be together yet, but darn it, Ellen. This company is a family. I want to get to know your young man, I want to be involved. That's why I want the two of you to make sure and come to the company barbecue on Saturday. No,'' he said, holding up his hand when Ellen opened her mouth to speak. ''I won't take no for an answer. Not at all. But that's not what I called you in here for.''

Ellen released a small sigh of relief. Josh squeezed her hand reassuringly, and she found she was breathing hard. Probably the tension of waiting for Mr. Tarenton to get to the point.

''The point is,'' her boss said, pacing again, turning to grin at them. ''I told Mrs. T. about the two of you and how this young man sent you one of our prime koalas. Told her what a romantic son of a gun you've got here, Ellen. And she suggested—I think you're going to love this—she suggested that we have the wedding at the Tarenton family homestead. She knows that since your mom's death you don't have a woman who's older and wiser to help you with the arrangements, Ellen, and you know we don't have any daughters. Nothing would make us happier than to have one of our own married on our grounds. Beautiful place, Hawthorne. You'll see it Saturday when you come. What do you think, Ellen? How's that sound? How would you like to make this a real Tarenton wedding?''

Ellen jerked. She realized that she was probably crushing the bones in Josh's fingers, she was gripping his hand so tightly. She turned to him, opened her mouth, then closed it again, unable to speak as disappointment and panic rushed over her.

''The wedding?'' she finally said, her voice a weak thread. ''I—''

''That's extremely generous of you, Mr. Tarenton,''

Josh said smoothly. "Ellen and I never imagined that you'd take such a personal interest in our relationship."

Concern for the man sitting beside her took precedence over all else in that instant. Josh had just been trying to help her, now he was being pushed into a corner. Things were moving along like a train with no brakes. Her own disappointment over the fact that she hadn't gotten the promotion wasn't something she could think of. Not yet, anyway.

"Mr. Tarenton," she began, holding out one hand. "That's so very kind of you and Mrs. Tarenton, but Josh and I really haven't even discussed dates for the wedding yet. We've been apart for so long—"

Mr. Tarenton's bushy brows came together. "Not having second thoughts, are you? Have you found out this young man was unfaithful while you were apart? Something like that?"

Second thoughts? She was wondering what on earth had ever possessed her to begin such a crazy and ill-advised scheme. Why had she believed she could play this kind of game when she'd never been very good at playing games, anyway? Still, Mr. Tarenton's implication that Josh had been less than honorable rankled. A lot.

"Josh *has* dated a number of women, Mr. Tarenton. Of course, he has. He's gorgeous. But he would never cheat on the woman he is currently with," she said, her voice gently reprimanding. "He's a very honorable man."

"We haven't made any plans because—well, heck, we've just been too involved in the thrill of being together and getting to know each other again to think beyond the moment," Josh said, gazing into her eyes as if he was truly looking at a woman whom he planned to get to know very well. "Still, your wife must be quite a lady to offer to help us, Mr. Tarenton. We'll try to give her a date as soon as possible.''

"That's good, then. That's wonderful," Mr. Tarenton agreed. "And, Ellen, I'm sorry if it seemed I was insulting the man you love. I see now how you shame people who shirk their jobs into getting back to work. For a second there, I almost felt guilty. Thought I was going to have to write you up for insubordination."

He chuckled and nodded, signaling the end of the conversation. As Ellen stepped to the door, she turned to see Josh look straight at her boss.

"We'll be at that barbecue with bells on, Mr. Tarenton. Wouldn't miss it."

As she and Josh walked back out into the office and she escorted him to the door, she counted to twenty. Slowly.

Standing next to the heavy plate glass doors that divided Tarenton employees from the world, she stopped, staring up at Josh.

"I'm sure I could have thought of an excuse to beg off on Saturday," she said, frowning up at him. "It could be difficult keeping up this charade for an entire day."

"Ellen," he said, sliding his hand behind her neck and his fingers beneath her hair in an intimate gesture "It's a party, Ellen. Don't you ever take time off just to have fun?"

"Sometimes," she conceded, though she honestly couldn't remember the last party she'd attended. "But this one—"

"Is going to afford us the perfect opportunity to show your boss that you're truly part of his family now. This is going to speed things along. He's going to realize by the end of the day that we're truly in love. No way am I going to have my constancy questioned again," he said, with a mocking smile, staring directly into her eyes. "By the way, thank you for defending me," he whispered. "But you shouldn't have bothered. There's no way anyone is going to think I have time or thoughts for anyone else but you. I intend to make very sure of that, Ellen. You can count on it. And I'm sorry that the news wasn't better."

She shrugged. "I guess I shouldn't have thought things would happen so fast. I shouldn't have gotten my hopes up so soon."

"Shhh," Josh whispered. "I understand what it's like to want something, to wish things would happen fast. Don't feel foolish about that. And don't worry," he said, smoothing his fingers down her eyelids with his other hand, soothing the worry lines from between her lids.

In the next instant she felt herself being drawn up. She braced her hands on Josh's shoulders to keep herself from falling. Then his mouth was on hers, his warmth was all around her. And this was no gentle kiss between friends. This was heat and passion, his lips slanting over hers, covering her, drawing her closer, tasting her and offering her to taste the heat of his mouth. His body was closer than close—but not close enough. Ellen's hands twined about Josh's neck. His arms slid around her, lifting her. She felt her toes curl, and one shoe slipped off her foot. The world was spinning, all sensation concentrated in the heat of Josh's mouth, in her breasts, in the molten warmth between her thighs.

And then he lowered her gently to the ground, holding her until she found her balance. Josh cleared his throat.

"I'll see you later," he promised, just before he went out the door.

She was left standing there, one shoe off, her lips burning and swollen, her every sense spinning.

Had she really thought that everything would be fine less than an hour ago? What a fool she'd been then. Mrs. Tarenton was planning a wedding that would never be. Mr. Tarenton was pulling her and Josh in much deeper than she'd ever planned to go. Josh was sacrificing more of his free time than she'd ever meant to accept. He was proving to be much better at acting than she had ever imagined…and she was beginning to realize that she was no actress at all.

She had taken part in that kiss heart and soul. Even knowing that it was just for show, she'd closed her eyes and lost herself to reality with more fervor than she'd ever done anything else before.

If Josh kissed her again—and he would, of course he would, it was part of the dangerous game they were playing—there was no way she ever wanted him to know that her passion had been real. He'd kissed a thousand women. She didn't want to be another one of those ladies who spent their lives waiting for his phone call, or his touch.

She didn't want to be anyone's woman, especially not Josh's. And she wouldn't be. She'd been caught off guard this time; she hadn't been prepared for the shock of his skin against hers. But next time she would be ready, she'd have her guard up.

And she would not feel. The next time he touched her, she'd be pretending—just the way that he was.

Chapter Four

Something was definitely wrong with this picture, Josh thought, as he pulled up to Ellen's apartment building on the day of the barbecue. Yeah, he thought, staring at the clock on the dash. Something *was* wrong, and it didn't take a member of Mensa to figure it out. He was fifteen minutes early.

Josh Hawthorne was never early. For anything.

Must be the thought of all that barbecue. Maybe he was just hungry, he decided, leaning on the wall outside Ellen's doorway as he rang the bell.

Two seconds later the door slid open. Ellen looked out, cautiously, confused. She smiled at him, her head tilting in that cute little way she had.

"Josh," she said with surprise, her voice soft and sweetly hesitant.

Oh, yeah, he was hungry. Too bad it wasn't for barbecue.

The thought slipped right in there where it didn't belong. No point in denying it, though. He'd been craving another taste of Ellen's lips ever since that searing and totally out-of-control kiss in her office the other day. And what he had in mind was more than staged embraces, well-rehearsed touches. Oh, yes, he'd definitely been wanting more. Ellen's pale arms wrapped around his neck, her silver-blue eyes gazing up at him from his pillow. He wanted Ellen Rhoades—all night, no witnesses this time.

And she didn't want any of that. She didn't want any entanglements, nothing but her promotion.

Too bad. It was a damned appealing fantasy, one that was taking wings now that he was standing here and realizing that he had caught her fresh out of the shower. Her V-neck robe was clinging. A trickle of water she'd missed tracked down her temple, her cheek, pooled in the hollow of her neck, urging him to lean forward and stroke away the silvery wetness, to press his lips to her pale, trembling skin.

Josh cleared his throat. He leaned one hand against the door frame.

"I'm early," he commented, his voice crusty and hoarse. "So there's plenty of time, Ellen. Don't go getting that purposeful, 'let's get down to business and get this done' look you wear so well. And don't you dare rush around trying to get yourself dressed in a hurry."

He shouldn't have said that. She obviously felt self-conscious about her half-dressed state. Wrapping her bathrobe more tightly around her to close the tiny gap that revealed only a slender wedge of creamy skin, she only succeeded in outlining her body more clearly, making her hips and breasts even more visible and tempting.

Josh closed his eyes, took a long, slow breath. No big deal, he reminded himself. This was just desire. Familiar. Strong. He'd felt it before—many times. Not this pressing, not this consuming, but he knew the taunting taste of the stuff, knew it was fleeting. It would pass if he ignored it.

A door opened and closed down the hallway, and Ellen raised her head quickly.

"I'm sorry. Come in," she said, stepping back to allow him room to brush past her.

He did so carefully. Real carefully. Their bodies didn't touch.

When the door closed behind him, Josh felt as if the air had been sucked out of the room. Ellen was only inches away, her hair slipping out of the loose knot on her head, damp tendrils kissing her neck. Bare pink toes peeped out from beneath the fluffy white chenille of her robe. His imagination wandered underneath the hem, up the sweet length of her legs.

Damn! There was a reason he was never early, Josh reminded himself. If he'd been late as usual, he wouldn't be standing here with her like this. She'd be dressed, she wouldn't be so self-conscious—and he wouldn't be acting like a foolish teenager trying to sneak a peek at what he had no business wanting to see. He'd promised to help the lady, show her how to relax. And what woman in her right mind could relax when there was a male flaring his nostrils like a deprived stallion standing in her living room?

The thought brought Josh up short. He stared into Ellen's blue eyes and realized that for all the woman could work company miracles, she was still a babe in arms where men were concerned. He felt a sudden urge to hold her, protect her—from himself and anyone like him.

He couldn't help offering her a gentle smile then, trying to make her see that he would never hurt her.

"Ready to go kick up your heels today?" he asked soothingly. "Smear some barbecue sauce on your chin? Lounge around in the sun and just be lazy?"

His reward was a spark of sunshine that appeared in her blue eyes.

"If you think I'm going to walk around with a messy face in front of my boss, Josh Hawthorne," she said, shaking her head and grinning, "then you must not know me very well."

Oh, but he did. He did. At least he knew that Ellen really would have trouble letting herself relax today. And he also knew that he was going to make it his business to ensure that she had a good time. After the way he'd watched her soothe that inventor's ruffled feathers the other day, the way she'd personally handled crisis after crisis, Josh knew that she was a real asset to Tarenton. She deserved a day of fun in the sun—but she wouldn't reach out and take it. That wasn't her style. Unless she was forced to the wall.

"I don't know, Ellen," Josh said, rolling his eyes. "Might be bad policy not to take off your corset today. Mr. T. and his wife have obviously gone to great lengths to arrange this day. They're going to expect a little co-operation."

Ellen crossed her arms over her chest, hiding some of Josh's favorite parts. Concentration furrowed her brow— before an impish grin lifted her lips.

"I knew this was a bad idea," she teased. "You're just trying to get my nose out of those books again, aren't you?"

He grinned back at her, leaning against the door lazily. "And what if I am?"

"My job's at stake here," she reminded him, softly.

"No." He shook his head. "Tarenton's no fool. Your

job's not at stake, but something is. All work and no play, Ellen…'' He let the words trail off. ''Tarenton wants to see you as a person, a woman who wants a life and a family, not just a highly prized employee,'' he reminded her. ''I'm not here to show him how well you can do your job.''

At his final words, Ellen shifted, she took a deep breath, biting her lip. ''You're here to help me,'' she said, as if speaking to herself. ''But I didn't anticipate that you'd have to be putting in so many hours when I agreed to this. It's Saturday,'' she mused. ''You should be getting some time off.''

''Ellen, there's no need to feel guilty. In the hours I'm not with you, I have plenty of time for myself and my work. Europe is only a continent away, and it's amazing what a guy can accomplish in this day of computers, modems and fax machines. But you're right about one thing. I should be having a good time,'' he agreed. ''And I intend to. With you. At the party,'' he reminded her, turning her gently and pushing her toward the doorway that obviously led to her bedroom. ''Go get dressed now,'' he urged. ''And wear something you can roll around in the grass in.''

She paused at that, his hand resting against the small of her back. An inch lower and his fingertips would skim the swell of her perfect little fanny. For a second the clock stopped ticking, Josh thought. Or maybe it was just that the sudden roaring in his ears stilled all other sound.

Ellen's sudden deep breath pressed her more firmly against him. She stepped away, peeking back over her shoulder.

''I want you to enjoy yourself,'' she agreed. ''But just don't expect miracles, Josh. I'm not like Penny, not nearly as casual. There's a limit to how much I can let down my hair in what is still essentially a business atmosphere.''

"Okay," he said reassuringly. "If it will make you feel better, I promise I won't insist that you lick your fingers clean. You can use a napkin."

A low, feminine chuckle trailed behind her as she continued on her way. "You're terrible, Josh. You always were," she reminded him as she went on her way.

No, Josh thought, trying not to listen for the sounds of Ellen shedding her clothes. In the past he'd been incorrigible, a tease, a man who lived only for fun and didn't care who knew it. Only lately, when he'd started to lust after a woman who didn't want his lust, had he become terrible.

He was just going to have to do something about that. Today he would do his best to think of Ellen in the old way: a cute little sister, a friend he wanted to have some fun with, a woman he was helping with a problem that just happened to involve a fair amount of physical contact.

That would do it. That would be fine. If he thought of Ellen that way, then he could touch her without wanting to take things a step farther.

Then he could get through this day without embarrassing the lady in front of her colleagues.

All right, so maybe she wasn't dressed as casually as Josh would have liked, Ellen thought, stepping out of his car at the Tarenton estate. She'd seen it in his eyes the second she moved out of her bedroom and into his line of vision.

Her dress was summer yellow, cotton—but still a dress. And not a let's-have-fun dress like the loose Western-style skirts some of the women were wearing. Not jeans and a blouse, either. She was dressed simply, suitably, but no way did she look like she was ready to throw caution to the wind.

"You're beautiful," Josh said, and Ellen felt a sweet thrill run through her, one she quickly squelched.

Just because she had stepped out of character to play a risky game didn't mean she'd changed. She was still the same stubbornly serious and basically up-front person she'd always been, and she was happy to be that way. She didn't want Josh to offer her what he'd offered other women so many times. She didn't need pretty lies. No, what she wanted from Josh was…well, she didn't know. She'd only meant to borrow his name for a time, had never dreamed he'd show up in the flesh and champion her cause. Now that he was here, she wasn't sure what to do, how to act, but she knew darn well what she *didn't* want. She desperately didn't want to let her guard down, to like him too much. No way did she want him to think she needed or expected flattery, and wasn't that exactly what he was doing? Definitely. Of course.

But when she turned to tell him her thoughts, she stared up into those smoky amber eyes and saw not kind condescension, but—honesty, admiration and…a hint of something else, something fierce and elemental. Her words locked up, frozen in her chest.

"Thank you, Josh," she finally managed.

"Come on," he said, sliding his hand beneath her arm. "We'd better report in right away, attend to the formalities before we get down to the business of smothering ourselves with fun. I know you'd be mortified if you had to face the Tarentons with dirt on your chin or grass stains on that pretty yellow dress."

She looked up quickly to see if Josh was serious—but of course he wasn't. Josh was rarely serious.

"I'm ready," Ellen agreed, resting her palm on his forearm, wishing she could summon up more conviction. In truth, she wasn't ready for this day at all. A whole day of pretending in front of the entire Tarenton family. An entire day of trying to make the world believe that she and Josh would be walking down the aisle in a few months.

Impossible.

But not *too* impossible, Ellen realized later. Josh had smoothly led her to the Tarentons' side. She'd smiled and chatted, accepting Hazel Tarenton's congratulations as if she really deserved them. This was getting way too easy, pretending to be Josh's intended.

"I'll let you know as soon as we set a date," she promised Mrs. Tarenton, glancing up at Josh for confirmation.

He was looking at her as though she were a delicious bit of fudge icing on a chocolate cake, as though he was having to steel himself not to gobble her up. Ellen took a deep breath, returning his glance—just for the Tarentons' sake, of course.

But when Josh finally leaned close and brushed the tip of one finger across her nose, she realized that she must have been standing like that for some time.

"They're gone," he whispered. "You were something else, sweetheart. Absolutely convincing."

Looking away quickly, Ellen gave herself a mental shake. She hoped she hadn't looked too convincing. It was all too easy to remember her mother looking at her father as if he was the only thing in her world, just as he went out the door...again. That kind of all-consuming feeling had crippled her mother, made her almost useless to the children who needed her. It was certainly not the kind of emotion Ellen wanted to have anything to do with. She had a different plan for her life, something better, something good and lasting, something that was all her own.

She took a deep breath, determined to shake off her mood. Tilting her head up toward Josh, she raised one brow.

"I'm becoming a consummate liar, and you're praising me?" she muttered with a grin.

"Who said you were lying?" he argued. "All you said was that you would let Mrs. Tarenton know when we set our wedding date. The fact that you didn't also add that the chance of that happening was zero to the ninety-ninth power does not actually constitute a lie. Ask any ten-year-old boy," Josh argued, ending on a grin.

Ellen started to return his smile, then shook her head. "This has gotten so much more involved than I anticipated," she admitted.

Josh nodded, reached down and took her hand in his own, smoothing her skin with his thumb. "Don't start getting down on yourself, sweetheart," he warned. "Dealing with injustice is rarely clean-cut and easy. Now come on," he urged, tugging her forward. "Let's go eat. And Ellen?"

She looked up. "Yes?"

"I hear there's going to be a greased pig contest later," Josh said, his brows raised in challenge. "I dare you to catch one."

Ellen couldn't keep the twinkle from her eyes. "You're just saying that to get a rise out of me, Josh, but we'll see who has the last laugh. Because the world at large thinks I already *have* caught something just as challenging. Some of the girls you used to date seemed to think you were as slippery as a greased pig, anyway. Or at least that's what they told me."

Josh's laugh was deep and masculine. It rolled over Ellen in waves, sending shivers of awareness down her body, right to her toes. Slipping off one shoe, she flexed her foot, trying to chase the sensation away.

Ten minutes later, she was seated beside Josh at a picnic table, their plates piled high with barbecue, potato salad and baked beans.

Giving her yellow dress a thorough study, Josh handed her a fistful of napkins.

Ellen rolled her eyes and relaxed a bit more. Josh *had* been right in his assessments of the Tarentons' expectations, after all. Today she was here to show she was a part of the family, that she fit in, and she was determined to ignore that niggling serious side of her that found it so difficult to relax. Josh was making a gallant effort for her sake. How could she do any less?

Looking down at the handful of napkins, Ellen shrugged. "I thought you wanted to get down and dirty," she said, getting into the spirit of things.

"We will, sweetheart. We will," Josh promised. "The day is still young." He reached over, took a corner of one napkin and found the bit of barbecue sauce she had missed with her tongue. Then he winked.

Ellen couldn't help it. She winked back. She picked up his own napkin and brushed at his upper lip, even though there was nothing there. At that moment, a sharp click snicked at her side, and she looked up to find a photographer giving her a nod.

"Oh, no, Mr. Tarenton wants pictures," she said on a groan.

Josh slid his arm around her waist, snugging her up against the lean warmth of his side. "Then we'll give him pictures, sweetheart." And he leaned down and gently brushed at her lips with his own.

It was a moment that the photographer missed.

But he didn't miss Josh trying to teach her the Texas Two-step out on the makeshift dance floor. He didn't miss the two of them feeding each other bites of pie at the baking demonstration Mrs. Tarenton had set up. In fact, there were times when Ellen felt as if the man with the camera was trailing them, as though they were the only people of interest at this jamboree. But she quickly pushed her worries aside. Josh was in his element here. He was a man who knew how to enjoy life to the hilt, and Ellen found that being his partner for the day was absolutely…exhilarating, seductive. She wondered if this was the way Penny had felt when she'd spent her three months with Josh, then quickly nudged the thought away. She wondered if Mr. Tarenton would let her have a few copies of those pictures.

"Having fun yet?" Josh leaned and whispered in her ear, his big palm resting on the curve of her waist.

She closed her eyes and nodded. He'd been touching her all day like this, his hands never straying far from her shoulder, her arm, the curve of her hip. Even if it was just for show, it was…nice.

"What's next?" she said, smiling, unwilling to open her eyes. The sensation of touch without sight was too exquisite, the sun too bright overhead.

She could feel Josh suck in a deep breath. A small shriek escaped her as she felt herself lifted off her feet.

"I've entered us in a race," he confided, holding her in his arms.

A low chuckle escaped her. Obviously this man didn't know squat about her athletic abilities. "Josh," she said, shaking her head sadly as she looped her arms around his neck to keep from falling. "If you're carrying me because you thought I'd object to this great idea of yours, you're right. Have you ever seen me run?''

Josh stared down at the woman whose face was so close to his. She was beautiful, a slight trace of sunburn on her nose, her oh so carefully combed hair flying wild around her face after a day of partying. Had he ever seen her run? In a race, never. But he'd seen the lady run from other things. Yes, he had.

''Are you trying to tell me that after you've been so game all day, you're going to back out on me now?'' he teased.

''I run like a duck,'' she whispered. ''The miracle lady of Tarenton Toys can work wonders with numbers, with personnel, with schedules, but I run like a duck.'' She smiled at him then, obviously not really ashamed of this deficiency of hers. After all, she *was* the miracle lady of Tarenton Toys. What did she have to be ashamed of? ''Still want to see me run?'' she asked, wrinkling her nose at him.

Josh beamed down at her as he made his way to the starting line. ''Well, sweetheart, I admit that I really would like to put your theory to the test someday, but that won't be necessary right now. You see, in *this* race, I get to carry you.''

And at that, a starting gun sounded. Josh took off just as Ellen sat up in his arms, struggling to see what was going on around her.

''Ellen, could you just be a bit more still?'' He choked out the question, as her weight, light though it was, shifted, nearly throwing him off balance.

''You could have told me,'' she said, continuing to sit ramrod straight. ''Hasn't anyone complained that this is a bit chauvinistic? I mean Tarenton Toys isn't on the cutting edge of female empowerment, but still—''

"Well *you* could have carried *me,* Ellen, but I think that would have been just a tad difficult in this case," Josh managed to say, nodding to two other couples who had reversed positions and were being cheered on by the crowd. "I'm sure I outweigh you by more than a few pounds."

His reference to the other couples seemed to have stilled her, for Ellen sat back in his arms after that. She pulled herself in tighter, closer to him, making it harder for him to think straight but easier for him to move. When he collapsed on the grass at the finish line two lengths behind another couple and still cradling her close, Ellen planted a light kiss on his cheek.

"I'm sure you could have won if you hadn't eaten all that barbecue," she told him, giving him an impish grin.

Laughter welled up inside of Josh as he stared down at the gorgeous, infuriating bundle of woman snuggled close to him. She knew darn well that it was the distraction of her movements that had cost him this race. She also knew that it didn't matter a whit to him.

"You're one very game lady, Ellen Rhoades," he admitted, brushing her cheek with one finger.

"Thank you. And thank you for the party, too, Josh," she said. "This was fun. Next time I might even enter the greased pig contest."

Laughing into each other's eyes, Josh heard the identifying click of the camera—and was immediately reminded of just what had brought him to this place, this time.

It bugged the heck out of him to think that he had Hugh Tarenton to thank for this day. The man had found a gem in Ellen, had probably known it the day she first walked into his office. The fact that he'd held back her reward like the proverbial carrot on the stick was a crime.

   And after today Josh was more determined than ever
to make Tarenton change his mind and right his wrongs:
fast. He wasn't sure he could take too many more epi-
sodes of Ellen in his arms without making some seriously
stupid moves.

Chapter Five

She'd forgotten how enticingly seductive Josh could be, how easily he could make a person smile—or then again, maybe she hadn't. It was just something she'd never really wanted to acknowledge, Ellen admitted, studying him from the shadowed passenger side of the car as they drove home from the barbecue.

In truth, her heart had skipped several long and lasting beats the first time Penny had ever brought him back to the apartment. And that had been scary. Really scary. Because that was the way every other woman she knew reacted to Josh, and Ellen knew the dangers of that kind of mind-numbing hero worship. So she'd fought, buried her nose deep in her books. She'd done her best not to notice golden-eyed, golden-tongued, live-for-the-millisecond Josh Hawthorne. She had goals, she needed to stay focused, not spend her time waiting for the smiles of a man who had half the women on campus sighing over him.

But today, she'd forgotten all that for a while. She'd

lapped up Josh's laughter, reveled in his smiles and the attention he lavished her with. She'd almost forgotten that this was just a show, but...

"We're here. Home." Josh's low, deep voice slipped through the deepening darkness as he pulled his car up in front of her apartment and got out, moving to open her door.

When Ellen stood, she found herself face-to-face with Josh's chest, the soft cotton of his shirt, the shoulders she'd rested her head on several times today. The urge to continue the fantasy for just a few moments longer was there and...definitely appealing.

He'd play along, she knew that. They were still outside, still in the public arena.

Ellen closed her eyes, reason battling with rich desire. Pitting will against want, she swayed on her feet, imagining her cheek against his shirtfront, the cloth warm from his body, his heartbeat a drugging throb beneath her skin...

As though he'd read her mind, he leaned closer, his fingertips found her arm, brushed up her skin to stroke her neck beneath the sweep of her hair.

"Ellen?"

The soft, choking voice came out of the dark silence. Feminine. Not Josh.

Startled, still groggy with the sensations that had swirled around her seconds earlier, Ellen looked up into Josh's questing eyes. He steadied her with his other hand as they both turned toward the walkway to the apartment entrance. A young woman was rushing toward them.

"Ellen." The blond child-woman stopped six feet away beneath the gaslight at the edge of the walk. Unshed tears thickened her voice and misted her eyes as she clearly struggled to smile. "I—I'm really sorry I just popped in like this. I...didn't know you'd have company, but I—I needed, I mean I just thought you could—''

She raked her lip with her teeth, looking from Ellen to Josh and back again.

Ellen stepped forward automatically, as she had so many times, as she always would. ''It's all right, Lynn,'' she said gently. ''This is Josh Hawthorne, a—a friend of mine. Josh is helping me...work on getting my promotion,'' she explained lamely.

Trying to ignore the fact that Josh had placed one hand at her waist—and kept it there—Ellen looked up at him. ''Lynn is my sister,'' she explained.

Looking at Josh with sad eyes, Lynn aimed a slight, quivering smile in his direction. ''I'm—glad someone's helping Ellen,'' she said softly. ''I don't like Mr. Tarenton, not at all. Ellen's so good and smart and dependable. Every time Mom was—sick, Ellen was always able to take care of my brothers and me, and I'm sure she's even better at managing now that she's grown up. That man should acknowledge her. He just isn't fair. I hate injustice. It just makes me so mad when someone hurts someone else needlessly—''

Lynn broke off, thrusting up her chin and glancing at Josh as if she'd just remembered that he was there. ''I'm sorry, I'm a little upset right now. But—I—that is, I mean, I *didn't* mean to put an end to your date. Maybe I better just go home now,'' she said, twisting her fingers together anxiously.

Opening her mouth to protest, Ellen was stopped by a slow shake of Josh's head. ''Don't leave on my account. You weren't intruding,'' he soothed. ''I was just bringing your sister home to tuck her in, but I'll let you do that now. Nice meeting you, Lynn. Good night, Ellen. Sweetheart.''

And without another word, without even pulling her farther into the shadows and away from her baby sister's view, he covered Ellen's mouth with his own, he kissed her quickly, a firm kiss of possession for anyone who cared to look.

"I'll call you in the morning," he promised.

Ellen felt warmth rush through her even as she wondered if Lynn could see the blush that was surely suffusing her skin. She had told Lynn Josh was a friend. He had called her "sweetheart," persisting in the lie.

She opened her mouth to explain to her sister once Josh had driven away.

"Josh—he's—"

"Gorgeous, obviously mad about you," Lynn supplied wistfully. "He sure doesn't kiss like a friend, anyway, Ellen. Are you and he—"

Ellen put up one hand. "I'll explain later. Let's talk about you. I can tell that you've been crying. About Richard?" she asked, naming Lynn's soon to be ex-husband.

Lynn started to speak, she closed her mouth, nodded, tried again to find the words.

"I think—Ellen, I think I almost hate him right now," she said in a quick, broken whisper. "He must hate *me* to have said the things he said tonight."

She struggled for breath, opened her mouth again. A low, whispery moan came out.

Then her lips began to tremble. She covered her eyes as slow tears began to trickle through her fingers. Silently they came, like silvered raindrops in the moonlight. Awash with the misery she obviously couldn't hold back any longer, Lynn raised her face to Ellen as the teardrops slid down her cheeks and dropped onto her clothing, soaking the pink cotton.

She was a woman now. These were not the baby tears

that Ellen had once soothed away, but as Lynn lurched into her big sister's arms and hung on, her slight body shaking, Ellen knew that time and age would never make a difference in their relationship. Lynn would always be the child, Ellen the mother who needed to hold her and help her whenever she could.

"He came and asked for my wedding ring back, Ellie." Lynn choked out the words. "He said he wanted it for someone else." Her words ended on a moan that soon turned into helpless, jerking sobs.

Soothing her hand over her sister's thin back, Ellen willed her own tears not to fall. She wouldn't be any help at all to Lynn if she didn't seem strong herself. But Ellen couldn't keep the questions from forming in her mind. Why did all the Rhoades women seem to be attracted to men who were so very wrong, so inconstant and unreliable? Her mother had been that way, and Lynn and—

Ellen shut off the thought.

"Shhh, angel," she soothed, cooing to her sister, her baby, the youngest Rhoades child, the one Ellen had practically raised by herself. "Shhh, Lynn, he isn't worth your tears, not one of them," she said, unable to keep the anger from her voice.

"I know," Lynn sobbed. "I know, but—but I can't help it. I want to hate him, but I still love him. I wish he were different. I wish I could keep from caring or even thinking of him. I do."

Lynn looked up shyly as if she was ashamed at her words. "Do you understand, Ellie? Can you?"

Not exactly, Ellen thought. Lynn's husband had hurt her, failed her miserably, he had been wrong for her from the start and everyone had seen that except Lynn herself. Ellen couldn't really understand how Lynn could care for a man who was so bad for her, but—Ellen's thoughts turned to Josh, a just-for-the-moment man who was all wrong for a woman like herself, a man she'd never wanted to like or even notice.

"I think maybe I'm beginning to understand a little, Lynn," she promised.

She *was* beginning to understand—and she didn't like what she understood. Not at all. Because if she wasn't very careful, if she didn't tread softly, keep her mind on her goals and not on Josh, she could end up like Lynn. Strong, capable Ellen, the rock of her family, the one who never shattered, could still be hurt. She could lose her dreams and all that she'd worked for if she—

But there were no ifs to consider, Ellen insisted, hugging Lynn close, offering the meager comfort of sisterly love. Because Ellen had seen the dangers, and she was ready. She would never allow herself to become yet another heartbroken Rhoades woman.

He was getting used to being known as Ellen's fiancé, Josh thought as he made his way to her place the next morning. Hell, who was he kidding? He was beginning to *like* all the perks that such a position included. Perks such as kissing her whenever and wherever he pleased.

The problem was that "whenever and wherever" was becoming all too often. He could barely keep his hands off her anymore. The feel of her soft, sweet lips beneath his own was just too damned appealing. Somewhere along the way he'd moved from helping Ellen to helping himself *to* Ellen.

"Hell!" Josh let out his breath in a deep rush as he pulled into the parking spot next to Ellen's car.

Only yesterday he'd been complaining about Tarenton taking advantage of Ellen's goodness. So what business did he have doing the same thing? She was not here for his pleasure. She had not asked for his help. He was darn well going to have to work harder not to abuse the privileges this unusual situation allowed. Kissing Ellen repeatedly was just way too easy on the lips and the nerve endings. He needed to remind himself—constantly—that this time with her wasn't real.

But when he got to her apartment three minutes later, all thoughts of reminding himself of anything faded away. She was already waiting for him, the door pulled back wide. Josh remembered that it was Ellen who had called him, not the other way around. Something must be up.

"Do you mind if we go somewhere where we don't have to worry about being seen?" she asked, hesitantly, looking up into his face.

Josh cocked his head toward the door of her apartment.

A rosy glow brightened her cheeks as she shook her head. "I know a park not too far away, within walking distance. It's a little run-down and no one much goes there, but I like it. We won't run into anyone from Tarenton, I'm sure."

Okay, so she was nervous about having him in her apartment. He supposed he deserved that, after he'd surprised her with that parting embrace last night.

"Sure, lead on—Ellen." Purposely he dropped the endearment he'd grown to associate with her, the one that suited her so well.

He smiled down on the top of her shiny brown hair as she assumed a no-nonsense gait that would lead them quickly to wherever it was that she wanted to go.

"So you *do* own a pair of jeans," he teased, studying the way the soft denim molded to her legs as he easily matched his stride to hers.

The air of tension slid out of her, and she looked up

at him, wrinkling her nose. "I'm a career woman, Josh, but I have real clothes like real people. I don't wear those tailored suits twenty-four hours a day. I don't sleep in them."

He raised one brow, lifted the corner of his lips.

"And don't you dare pull a Josh Hawthorne and ask what I *do* sleep in," she commanded, coloring brightly, even as she continued on in her hasty march to the park.

"Ellen," he drawled. "I wasn't going to ask that." And he *wasn't.* He'd bitten down hard on the inside of his jaw just to keep the words from slipping out. Not that he didn't want to know. He'd surely like nothing better than to see Ellen dressed—or undressed—in whatever she wore to bed. But he'd promised himself to try to behave a bit more the way she obviously wanted him to behave. He was trying. Oh, yeah, he was definitely trying. Still, it was going to take a mountain of effort to keep from teasing the lady. She looked so absolutely delicious when she blushed at his remarks.

"T-shirts," she said suddenly, frowning up at him as if she knew what he'd been thinking. "Long ones, down to the knee."

But not below the knee, Josh thought. And even a long T-shirt would be loose, it would lift easily, allowing easy access to all the cream and pink beneath it....

Damning his errant thoughts, Josh began that litany of law cases again. They were dull, they were boring, but anything was better than walking down the street letting Ellen and all of creation see the living evidence that her presence was having an obvious effect on his libido.

"Where is this park, anyway?" he asked, when the repetition whirling through his mind didn't have the desired effect.

"Half a block more." Ellen motioned down the street.

Josh looked in the direction she indicated. As they drew nearer, he saw that the place was, as she had mentioned, a bit run-down. The flower beds were sparse and slightly weedy, the small fountain flanked by benches had a hairline crack running down its length. But there were plenty of twittering sparrows and a few sunny patches of grass.

Motioning Ellen to a bench, he forced himself to sit several feet away.

"You've got something serious you want to discuss?" Of course she did. Ellen was almost always serious.

She nodded, turning to look him full in the face. "About last night. My sister—"

He met her gaze full on. Of course she was worried about her sister, the young lady with the tear-dampened eyes. She'd been genuinely distressed, and it had been obvious that there was a deep bond between the two. Naturally Ellen would be concerned, she'd want to help. Maybe she'd even *need* help if this was a truly serious situation.

"Your sister—is she all right?" he asked, reaching out to take Ellen's hand, to offer comfort. "Is there anything I can do to be of assistance?"

Ellen looked down at where their two hands were joined, she raised her face, blinking hard as a slow, sad smile crossed her lips.

"Josh," she said, shaking her head. "It's nice of you to offer, but you're already helping enough, and…there's really nothing you can do, anyway. Lynn's going through a divorce, a tough one. She met and married the wrong man, he broke her heart. It's as simple and as unfixable as that. There's nothing anyone can do, nothing I can do, except be there for her."

"All right." He drawled the words out slowly, a question in his tone. "Then if you don't want my help, then—"

"Then why are we here?" she asked, finishing his statement for him.

"Yes. Why are we here?" he repeated. "You mentioned your sister. I thought—"

"Last night," Ellen began, cutting in, "I was prepared to tell Lynn the truth about us. You and I," she clarified. "I didn't want to lie to her. But then you—"

"Didn't play fair," he said with a rueful smile. "I kicked sand on your castle, spoiled your plans. I kissed you like a lover right in front of your baby sister that you didn't want to deceive. And now you want to slap my face. Only Ellen Rhoades would never do such a thing publicly. All right, then," he said, holding out his hands in defeat and turning his jaw to one side. "I deserve your anger, Ellen. Go ahead. We're perfectly private."

"Thank goodness," she said, her voice a low, admonishing caress. Ellen did reach out then. She cupped his jaw lightly, coaxing him back to a more natural position. "I most certainly wouldn't want someone seeing the great Josh Hawthorne presenting his face to be slapped, and I hope you know that I would never do such a thing even if you deserved it, which I don't think you do. You may not know it, but you were right last night. I was wrong."

Josh turned his head a touch more, bringing his lips closer to Ellen's hand still resting on his jaw. Quickly she pulled her fingers away, cradling them in her other hand as though his touch had hurt her. Looking into her eyes, Josh studied her expression.

"How were you wrong, Ellen?" He deserved that slap, he knew he did. And only Ellen could have wrung that concession from him. He'd certainly never presented his face for punishment ever before, and he'd definitely done worse things. He'd broken hearts, breezed in and out of women's lives like a fickle wind.

Ellen took a deep breath. She pasted on that ultraserious expression that was so effective in the office, so endearing to him. "Lynn's hurting right now. Really hurting," she confessed. "She's always needed me. Our parents—well, my father was not a particularly good father. He was a terrible husband, unfaithful, not there half the time. My mother took it hard, she wasn't available much of the time when Lynn was growing up. Lynn looked to me instead. Now, more than ever, she needs me to be strong for her. I didn't want to lie to her, I *don't* want to lie to her, but when I tried to explain the situation to her after you left, well I ended up caving in, telling her that you and I *were* thinking of marrying. I couldn't see any other way. If she thought I was having troubles of my own, that they were deepening, getting more complicated and frustrating…"

Her voice trailing off, Ellen held out her hands, as though she were looking for the words to finish.

"She wouldn't turn to you?" Josh offered.

"No." Ellen shook her head. "Not that. She still would, but—I—it's just that, Lynn needs someone to lean on and I've always been that someone, the one person she could absolutely depend upon. If she knew exactly what you and I were involved in, well…" Ellen managed a small smile. "You have to admit that this plan I've put in action is more than a little shaky. It's certainly not the kind of thing I've ever done before. I just don't want Lynn to have worries heaped on top of her other worries."

"Like the worries you're having heaped on top of your own?" he asked.

A tiny spark flashed in Ellen's eyes. "I know what I'm doing," she insisted. "I'm choosing this way. Lynn isn't taking advantage of me. And that's not what I came to talk about, anyway. I just wanted to let you know that, as far as we can, you and I that is, I'd like to keep this story we've created as small as possible."

Josh was going to ask what exactly she meant by that, but the telltale flush was already spreading up her creamy throat.

"You want me to keep my hands off you from now on."

She sucked in her lip, and looked up at him with those big blue eyes. "I just don't think anyone but the people at Tarenton Toys needs to be convinced that much."

"And it's got to be embarrassing having your baby sister seeing you lip-locked with a man who obviously has designs on your body?" he offered, grinning openly.

"Well, I *am* almost like a mother to her," Ellen conceded. "And my brothers…"

Ellen's voice softened when she said the word "brothers."

"Did you raise them, too, Ellen? Are they their 'someone to lean on' as well as Lynn's?"

She looked up, defensively, stubborn, her jaw set. Josh could just see how she would handle an errant employee.

"I love them, too," she admonished. "I'm their sister, and I'm the oldest."

Ellen didn't have to add the rest. Knowing the way she was, her sense of responsibility, her dedication, he knew that she had been mother to her brothers as well as to Lynn. She cared…and she was worried. *He* needed to make sure he didn't add to those worries, he needed to let her know that she didn't have to be a rock for *him* to lean on, that he wouldn't expect more than she could give.

Gently Josh reached out and lifted a fat strand of hair that had crept over Ellen's shoulder. The silky brown stuff flowed over his fingers, he stroked it.

"We'll do this your way," he agreed. "I won't grope you in front of your family. I'll be as proper as you could want any fiancé to be when your brothers and Lynn are around. I'll do my best not to place you in too many uncomfortable positions. Is that what we came here to talk about?" he coaxed.

She nodded, smiled sweetly. "Yes, mostly, but also I wanted to thank you. With the way the day ended I didn't really get a chance to thank you for yesterday. Mrs. Tarenton told me late in the afternoon that her husband said that hiring me was one of the smartest things he'd ever done. I don't have to tell you that your being here has made a big difference in my life at Tarenton."

Josh drank in her smile even as his resentment at Hugh Tarenton grew. "The man has been deliberately obtuse," he said, stating the obvious. "I don't doubt that you were always a wonderful employee, Ellen. And that man is crafty, he's manipulative, but if you tried to walk out of his business, with or without me, there'd be a hole in his company. He knows that, he wouldn't let you go. You don't have me to thank for opening his eyes, Ellen."

"I have you to thank for helping me force his hand," she insisted.

And that was what he was here for, Josh realized. It was what he had come for. Because he'd thought it would be fun, because he wanted a break from advising other men not much different from Hugh Tarenton. Was that why he was here now? Today? He didn't know. He sure as hell didn't want to examine his motives too closely, but one thing was certain: It would be best for Ellen, best for everyone, himself included, if they brought this whole episode to a close quickly.

"Then let's force his hand," he agreed. "Let's storm the walls of Tarenton Toys. Let's get in Hugh Tarenton's face day and night, step up the pace, make him really believe that things are heating up between you and me. The sooner he believes this engagement is set in stone, that our marriage is inevitable, the sooner he's going to cough up that promotion."

Ellen took a deep, shaky breath. He knew what he was asking of her, that it wouldn't be easy for her to be on-stage almost all the time, with little time off to breathe and still manage to feel clean and honest, but he meant what he said. The sooner this was over and done, the sooner she could...be gone.

The sooner *he* could get as far away from the temptation Ellen offered as possible.

"Okay," she agreed. "You're the expert at creating a romantic mood. I trust you. I defer to your superior experience. You call the shots, but...not around my family. Around Lynn and my brothers..."

"Around Lynn and your brothers, Ellen, our relationship will be as pure as Ivory soap. No lips, no tongues, not even my arms around you. Just some good old-fashioned hand-holding. Nothing more exciting than that."

It was a promise he meant to keep. Too bad the thought of simply holding Ellen's hand was giving him the shakes. If he didn't watch himself, he'd end up falling in love with Ellen Rhoades.

It was a stupid thought. Completely idiotic. He'd never been known to fall in love before—not for more than a few minutes at a time, anyway.

And Ellen was not a woman who wanted love. He wouldn't ask her to give him what she didn't want to give, not when so many other people were asking so much of her already. Not when he could never give back.

Chapter Six

Ellen thunked her briefcase down on her desk and looked at the collection of eyes turned her way. She glanced down at her clothing. No, her panty hose weren't bagging around her ankles, all her buttons were in their buttonholes. No rips, no tears, she was pretty sure that the small amount of makeup she'd applied had not smeared.

"So where is he, Ellen?" Nissa Robards asked, sidling over to her desk. "Mr. Tarenton told us your Joshua had asked for a tour of the company today. So where'd you hide him?" The perky, petite blonde smiled broadly. "Could it be that he's not getting a full eight hours every night? Trying to spend so much time making up for all that time away from you that he's dropped off from sheer exhaustion?" she suggested.

Ellen rolled her eyes. If it had been anyone else talking, she might have thought such a comment was a bit mean. Coming from good-natured, I-have-no-secrets Nissa, however, the bluntness was just—Nissa. Still, Ellen was glad that Josh had called her to let her know he'd accepted the invitation for the tour today, to warn her. She should have known the news would raise a stir.

"He'll be here, Nissa," she said, smiling back and placing a reassuring hand on her friend's sleeve. "Don't worry, you'll get to ooh and aah over him all you want. Josh is just not a morning person."

Her comment caused Nissa's eyebrows to rise. Ellen wondered what her colleague would think if she told her that the only reason she knew that was because Penny had once invited Josh to watch the sun rise with her— and been laughingly informed that he was not fit for human viewing before eight-thirty, sometimes later. Instead Ellen had tagged along with Penny. They'd brought Josh a photo, which he'd promised to cherish—his closest encounter with a sunrise.

"What kind of a person is Josh, exactly?" another more breathy voice chimed in, snagging Ellen's attention back to the present.

She looked up at the shy-eyed brunette shuffling papers at her side.

The group at her desk was beginning to grow, Ellen noted with dismay. Well, what had she expected when she'd come in early today? For the past few days, ever since Josh's arrival, she'd purposely been sailing into the office at the very last minute. She hadn't wanted to answer any questions. Today, however, she'd thought she might be able to sneak in early, that if she clicked on her computer soon enough and dug into the stack of work on her desk, she'd discourage the curious. She'd planned on getting a few things done before she had to accompany Josh and Mr. Tarenton on the tour.

Obviously she must have been hallucinating, Ellen

thought, zeroing in on that determined grin on Nissa's face.

"Okay, Ellen," the little blonde said. "I know you've been avoiding all our questions, coming in here so late that there hasn't been time for any good gossip before the big T. swoops down on us. But now we've got plenty of time. A good—" Nissa looked at her watch. "Oh, maybe ten minutes before we have to get back to the daily grind. So start talking and go ahead and spill your guts. Now that we've met him in the living flesh, we want to know a few things about that stunning hunk of love you've pledged life and limb to."

"Definitely," her dark-haired friend agreed. "Tell us everything about him, all the wonderful, glorious details. Everything." The woman's eyes practically glowed. If Ellen hadn't known Karen better, she would have sworn the lady was going to pass out right on the spot. The fact that the woman was practically fainting over her memories of Josh made Ellen want to…flip Josh's picture over again so that Karen couldn't see. The thought was disturbing. She realized that she was frowning at a woman she'd shared many smiles with, many frustrations. Karen and she weren't close, but they *were* daytime friends, colleagues.

Ellen took a deep breath, concentrating on uncurling her nails from her palms, on trying to appear somewhat calm as Karen leaned closer, waiting.

All right, who was she kidding? Of course, her friends were curious. They'd worked with her for seven years and suddenly she'd pulled a fiancé from a hat like a magic rabbit. Only Josh was a hundred times better looking than any magician's rabbit. A thousand times sexier, her memory and Karen's expression told her.

And her friends wanted to know everything.

Only there *was* no everything. There was just a lot of nothing, Ellen reminded herself, pushing away the thought of how her senses started spinning every time the man came too close.

That didn't count, it wasn't real. That was just a one-sided reaction to the man—the same kind Karen was experiencing. And she had no more claim to Josh Hawthorne than any of these women standing here did. In a few weeks, he'd be gone, leaving only a memory. She needed to remember that—and not dig this hole she was creating too deep. There was always the danger that she'd never be able to crawl out.

"I—Josh and I were just—friends," she said simply. "I met him a long time ago. Now we're engaged." Ellen wondered at the protective feeling she had toward Josh. She didn't want anyone digging for details about him. She'd known that he'd always made hearts beat faster whenever he was around, but had women always pursued him this blatantly? "That's all," she insisted.

Nissa shook her head sadly. "Hey, Ellen, babe," she said. "You don't have to look so defensive. Even I know that there are some things that are just between a woman and her man. We're not asking you what kind of underwear your Josh wears or what he likes to talk about after a few hundred hours of lovemaking. Not our business." But Ellen noted that Karen looked a little disappointed at Nissa's comment.

"Nope, not at all," the woman continued. "I was thinking more along the lines of where does the man come from, how come we've only just heard of him lately, what's he do to make those white shirts fit so nice, what's his history, any interesting skeletons in his family? Does he *have* a family? Any good-looking brothers, cousins, uncles? Any man at all in his family who's looking for an affectionate, albeit domestically challenged woman like me for a night or two?''

Nissa ticked the questions off on her long red-nailed fingers. She stood there, smiling, waiting.

Ellen smiled back, slowly, grudgingly. "Nissa, you amaze me every time you open your mouth. Please, don't ever let anyone tell you that you don't have guts.''

"Does that mean you're not talking?''

It meant she wasn't talking. Not because she thought her colleagues' questions were too personal, although certainly some of them were. Ellen had no intention of running off at the mouth about Josh's personal affairs. But even had she wanted to, she realized—she couldn't have. She didn't know that much.

She knew what Penny had told her, what little she'd learned during Penny and Josh's short time together, but Penny was a loyal friend—to her and to everyone she knew. She didn't gossip about her friends, not unless she had an awfully good reason. So Ellen didn't know.

And she hadn't bothered to even ask him anything. She'd accepted his help, and hadn't even asked one kind question about Josh personally. Because?

Because the less she knew of Josh the easier it was to pretend he wasn't getting to her, that she wasn't falling under his spell like everyone else.

"Ladies," Ellen said, blowing out an impatient breath. "If you want to know all about Josh, then I suggest you go straight to the source. If he wants you to know something, he'll tell you. Josh is very—''

"Virile," Karen said on a breath, her eyes widening as she turned toward the door.

Ellen managed not to look too disgusted…she thought. "Josh is very friendly, very open," she said. *Especially to women. Josh had always had a soft spot in his heart for women—of all types.* It was part of what made him so very dangerous.

"And he's here, walking this way," Karen whispered with a shiver.

Ellen looked up and stared straight into Josh's eyes, as he moved toward her. He was, as Karen had said, virile. His dark hair was slightly shaggy. His white shirt and black pants fit him to perfection. He had a lazy, knowing grin that could make any woman's common sense slip right out the door.

"Looks like it's time for us to make like ladybugs and fly away home," Nissa whispered to the other women. "Don't worry, though, we'll be back," she said near Ellen's ear. "I'm still hoping to find out if he's got a brother or a friend my size. Besides, as soon as you set a date, Karen and I are going to give you the shower of showers. The most personal kind. Thought you'd like to be prepared, throw out all that white cotton underwear I'll bet you're harboring at home."

At Nissa's comment about the shower, Ellen sat up straighter. How big did she say she'd dug this hole so far? Never mind, it was getting deeper fast. What had Josh said to her once? That she needed to wade in and let the water rush over her head. Well, it appeared that she was doing a fine job of it. Looking at Josh as he neared her, knowing that her colleagues were planning on showering her with lacy negligees for a honeymoon that would never take place, Ellen felt very much like she was drowning—in warm, seductive water.

Pushing back from her desk, she ignored the warning signals going off in her head. What else could she do, after all?

"Hi," she said simply, almost shyly as Josh came up to her. "You made it."

He grinned, bent and touched his lips to hers, a simple kiss of hello that shouldn't have felt so sinfully rich and drugging.

"I missed you," he said, his voice low but nevertheless loud enough for anyone at the nearby desks to hear. "It's been too long since yesterday."

She was supposed to say she missed him, too, or something equally false and loverlike, but the fact was that she *had* missed him, even if they had only been apart for one night and a few hours this morning. And she couldn't say the words, knowing that they were, in fact, true. He was playing the game he'd been playing all of his adult life, the relationship game, and he was good at it. Awfully good.

She wasn't.

So, ignoring the truth about missing the man as well as the lovers' game she'd have to stammer her way through, Ellen leaned forward, as close to Josh's ear as she could get without actually touching him.

"The women in my office are asking a lot of questions about you," she confided, aiming for a safer, saner truth.

He studied her, staring down into her eyes as he leaned closer. "Are you saying that they're suspicious, that we haven't been convincing enough?"

As if he meant to alleviate that possible problem, Josh slid the back of his hand along the line of her jaw in a brief caress that was over almost before it had begun.

Ellen swallowed her gasp. She allowed herself to acknowledge just how potent Josh's nearness was. Heavens, she probably wouldn't even qualify as a bona fide, healthy woman if she didn't react to him somewhat. At least she wasn't acting totally foolish the way Karen was. Not yet, anyway.

"Ellen?" he asked, reminding her that he'd asked a question.

"No," she whispered. "It's not that they're not convinced. They are, and that's—I suppose that's the problem. I never thought this would be so involved. I *like* the people I work with, and deceiving them—well, now it's getting worse. My friends are planning on showering me with lingerie. They're really getting into this."

A slow smile twisted Josh's lips. "Did you think they wouldn't? Weddings always bring people out of the woodwork, sometimes people you'd thought had surely forgotten your very existence."

There was a touch, the barest hint, of cynicism in his words. Coming from Josh—laughing, teasing Josh—the emotion caught Ellen off guard, brought her up short.

"You sound like you've been to a great many weddings." No surprise, she was sure. He was a handsome man, and single. Of course he would be in great demand as a guest at weddings. But his words, his tone of voice, there was more there than he was revealing. If Ellen hadn't known better, she would have said that he sounded slightly wounded.

"I've been to my share of weddings. A few," he conceded, not really telling her what she wanted to know. "But don't worry, sweetheart. We won't let things get that far with us, and your friends will forgive you when they know your reasons for practicing this deception. After all, they all know what kind of man you're dealing with in Tarenton, don't they?"

They did, Ellen acknowledged with a nod. And she hoped that Josh was right, that her friends would feel the end justified the means in this case. Because Nissa and Karen and the others did know what kind of man Hugh Tarenton was.

And so did she. She also realized that her friends, in the end, would benefit if she managed to bring her boss kicking and screaming into the present no matter how she accomplished her goal.

"They *do* know," Ellen agreed.

And she herself knew something. She was going to get to know Josh. She would not be running away anymore. He had been good to her. He deserved a friend—a true friend.

From now on, if the man had secrets to keep, she wanted to keep them because they *were* his secrets, not because she knew nothing of the man she'd told the world she was marrying.

"So, are you ready to show me around?" Josh whispered, touching his cheek to Ellen's satiny hair as he leaned closer, waiting for her response. He didn't care if Tarenton was waiting, he didn't care if he'd told the man he would be ready ten minutes ago. No one was going anywhere until Ellen had a chance to psych herself for this encounter.

Things were heating up but good with all this talk of showers and wedding dates. Josh tried not to even think of Ellen opening presents filled with little lacy bits of nothing that he would never see her wear—or get to remove. It was understandable that she should be feeling a bit shaky right now when he was more than a bit unsettled himself. Justice, he knew, wasn't always pretty or easily won.

But he intended to see that she had her justice, and all the time she needed to get herself ready for this next round with Hugh Tarenton.

"Let's go. I'm ready," Ellen agreed, taking a deep breath and catching Josh off guard with her sudden smile. She stared him dead in the eye, raising her chin in that way she'd always had, pushing her slim shoulders back as if girding herself for battle. She looked like a woman prepared to take on an entire battalion of Tarentons if she had to.

Josh wondered if the lady knew just how much he'd always admired her determination to march to her own beat. He wondered if she realized how impressive and breathtaking she could be once she'd set her course and decided that there was no turning back.

Decked out in a pale turquoise belted suit that revealed a tiny waist and a hint of shapely, kissable knee when she moved, she was just as beautiful as the most voluptuous all-out-naked woman he'd ever bedded, Josh had to admit. Add to that a pair of honest blue eyes, lips that could curve into the sweetest smile on earth and an air of commitment capable of slaying dragons or errant supervisors and Ellen Rhoades was one hell of a dynamite woman, an alluring siren who tempted him in a way he'd never believed possible. She was also damn risky business when neither of them had much time or anything else to offer each other, Josh reminded himself.

Ellen had plans, big plans that didn't include him or any other man. And he, well he'd never been one to stick around long, not to mention the clients he needed to see face-to-face at some time in the future. This little episode with Ellen was very temporary. It *was* a charade, on both their parts. He needed to remember that, to remind himself. Constantly.

"All right, if you're sure you're up for this, then I'm all yours, sweetheart," he offered, pushing his disruptive thoughts aside. "If you're the same thorough Ellen Rhoades I used to tease for studying too hard, then you know this place like the inside of your bedroom closet, so let's go find the big man and prove to him that he hit absolute pay dirt when he hired you. You lead, and I'll just dance around and fill in the appropriate blanks whenever you need me to play my part. I'm hoping that your Mr. Tarenton has his eyes open today, that he's going to recognize that he can't afford *not* to promote you.''

Ellen leaned back and looked up into his eyes. She lifted one brow and smiled slowly. ''What exactly does dancing around and filling in the blanks entail, Josh?''

He placed his hands on her forearms, and turned her so that she was leaning back against him. Josh allowed himself to breathe in the fresh, soapy scent of her for a bare two seconds before he gave her a gentle push.

''We'll see, Ellen. We'll see. Just think of this as an adventure, one that's going to have a spectacular ending. Just do the things that you do best, that come naturally to you.''

For one brief moment she was in his arms, her nearness calling forth urges that he'd never act on in this lifetime.

The next minute she had filled her lungs with enervating air, her body brushing his as she readied herself. Then she grinned up over her shoulder at him.

''Okay, get ready to samba,'' she said.

Josh chuckled as he watched Ellen move into action. She was back in safe territory. This was a simple company tour. He understood that she gave them often, though not usually with Mr. Tarenton in tow. Still, even if her boss's presence made her nervous, she would shine, Josh knew. She would definitely twinkle like bright, new gold. He wondered that her boss hadn't already noticed how she glowed or maybe the man *had* noticed. Maybe Hugh Tarenton was just being selfish, not obtuse. If he sent his prize employee off to Phoenix, this office would be a little barer, a bit less productive. No doubt about it.

That was something to look for, to think about. If that

was the case, Ellen just might find herself in need of a good lawyer—for a while, anyway.

But if they were lucky, if he was persuasive, if he was half the dynamic attorney that he was supposed to be, Tarenton would be won over long before that. In a matter of days, maybe even hours.

In no time flat, Ellen would be right where she wanted to be, have the life she'd always wanted…one that didn't include a husband and children. For her future plans certainly didn't include Josh Hawthorne.

Chapter Seven

"Ellen, Josh, good to see you. Are we all set?" Tarenton asked as he stepped out of his office and looked at his watch.

"Sorry we're late," Josh said, apologizing only because he knew Ellen was normally as dependable as the sun and the moon. He wouldn't have her paying the price for his own laissez-faire attitude. "I'm sure you know what it's like when you've been apart from the woman you worship for more than a few hours. I wanted to see Ellen alone before she put on her corporate hat to give me this tour."

He turned his attention to Ellen who had managed not to blush too much this time. She gave him a small grateful smile, then turned to Tarenton.

"If you don't mind, we'll start with the factory end of the operation, then return to the offices later. Our clients always seem to enjoy the building blocks part of the tour best, and since Josh isn't looking to invest in Tarenton, he might prefer to simply see what it is that we actually produce and how we do that.''

Tarenton rocked back on his heels. ''Not interested in investing in Tarenton? Ellen, everyone who marries a Tarenton employee is investing in our future. They're making a commitment to the firm. But, well, we'll get into that later, once the marriage license is signed. And I suppose the nuts-and-bolts part of the operation *is* the most interesting part of the show. So, let's do it. Let's show Josh here what we're made of.''

With a slight nod of acquiescence and a proud set to her shoulders, Ellen started toward a set of doors at the back of the main office. Down a long hallway, through another set of doors, she led them into a huge white space flooded with machinery, workers and, of course, the product that Tarenton was so proud of.

''You'll need to put this on just as a precaution,'' Ellen said over the noise of the machinery. She handed Josh a hard hat, then donned one herself as Tarenton popped his own on his head.

Leading her group around the perimeter of the room, keeping them within the ''safe'' zone, indicated by lines on the floor, Ellen quoted statistics concerning the company's output, stores and earnings. She explained the purpose of each machine and exchanged a few friendly words with the operators and inspectors.

''This particular part of the operation deals with some of the smaller elements that we make,'' she said, extending her arm in a wide arc to encompass the entire building. ''We have another factory in Phoenix where we manufacture stuffed animals and other toys that entail a great deal of stitching and one in Ohio where such things as bicycles, skates and wagons are produced.

''This room,'' she explained, leading Josh to a large

offshoot of the main factory, "is one of my favorites. My youngest brother spent a summer working in the 'glitter room.'" Ellen motioned to a woman who was pouring heaping scoops of glitter over a tray filled with plastic tubes, filling them, pounding them down, then topping them off with another big scoop of the green spangled stuff. "All summer long, our house sparkled from all of the glitter that fell out of Doug's clothing. Hello, Lois," she called, smiling at the woman and stepping up to the table to help her while they talked. "How's your daughter? And Henry, are you taking care not to put too much weight on your foot while it's healing?" she asked the man at the next table when Lois had smiled back, proudly admitting that her daughter would be off to college soon.

Henry winked at Ellen and shifted his weight away from the apparently injured foot. "Am I keeping off my foot? Heck, I've got you to yell at me if I don't take care of myself, don't I? Afternoon, Mr. Tarenton," he said to the man who gave him a silent but approving nod just before Ellen said her goodbyes and moved on down the hall.

"Do you know everyone who works here and all of their personal business?" Josh asked, after she had stopped to talk to several other people. Leaning close, he waved his hand out over the large room and all of its many employees. "I thought you spent most of your time in the offices."

"These are my friends, Josh," Ellen explained, shrugging her shoulders. "It's no big deal to know who they are. That lady in the glitter room was Lois Davies, and she took care of my brother while he was here. She made sure he learned the ropes and didn't get into too much trouble. And Henry has been with the company for years. He always has a friendly word for a beginner like I once was. As for Alma Gray, the lady who was sealing all the boxes, I used to baby-sit her sons during my free hours when I first started here. Of course I know them and care about them.''

Her personal interest in her co-workers was apparently ''no big deal'' to Ellen, Josh thought, but he didn't see the same glow of true caring reflected in Hugh Tarenton's eyes. And this time he couldn't even criticize Tarenton—not without his own guilt rising. Ellen's knowledge of this company and the people who made their livings here made him realize just how little he'd ever known of his own holdings. He was a wealthy man who'd benefited from the profits of his father's corporate interests. There'd been plenty of people who'd worked to make the money that he called his own, yet he knew almost nothing of those people, not on a personal basis, anyway. So this time he couldn't criticize Tarenton for not knowing about Henry's foot or Lois Davies's daughter. But he could still admire Ellen. She was a wonder—she knew this company from the ground up—and she deserved Tarenton's praise and his promotion.

''You're an absolute treasure,'' he said, speaking his thoughts out loud, loud enough to reach Tarenton's ears, apparently. The man chuckled.

''Looks like this tour's over, Ellen,'' Tarenton said. ''Your Josh hasn't noticed anything but you for the last five minutes. Better take a break so he can look his fill.''

Ellen raised her head quickly. The yellow hard hat slipped low over her eyes and Josh smiled, tipping it back for her. ''I was paying attention,'' he said, reprimanding the man. ''Hanging on every word. Ellen knows it all, doesn't she?''

''Hmm, well she certainly does know the toy business,'' Tarenton conceded. ''But what about you? Do you

know any more than you did a couple of days ago? Have
you two made any progress on your plans? Set a date?
Started looking for a place to make your nest?''

That delicious glow suffused Ellen's cheeks, but the
slight trace of worry lines also molded her forehead. Josh
knew what she was thinking. If she got that promotion,
she'd be setting up her house in another city, another
state. If Tarenton was asking whether they'd found a
place in Midland, then…what the hell did that mean?

''I guess I haven't been too concerned about where we
live, Hugh,'' he said lazily, deciding that it was well past
the time to become less formal with this bullheaded man.
It was time to make a few things perfectly clear. ''Personally I could settle down with Ellen anywhere—a
closet, a boxcar, a shack. Anyplace that has four walls
and, well, I can be pretty portable. It's Ellen's choice.''

There. He'd made it clear that Phoenix would be just
fine. No point in letting the man think that he would stand
between Ellen and her job.

Tarenton eyed him oddly, tilted his head. ''Interesting,
Hawthorne. Interesting. It sure as hell is a different world
these days, isn't it? Not too many old-school types left,
not many like my new man, Dennis Jarrod, and his wife.
She's trailed him around the country and back. Yeah,
Jarrod's young, but he's raring to go. Has a wife who's
willing to follow him, too. Interesting how different two
couples can be. Both young, but one old-fashioned and
one twentieth-century radical.''

A flare of anger surged forth in Josh. He tamped it
down, would study it later. So Tarenton wasn't going to
be such an easy sell, after all, was he? Who in hell was
this Jarrod guy, anyway? Obviously someone more suited
to Tarenton's image than Ellen was.

Josh felt Ellen's presence at his side rather than saw

it. He didn't take his eyes off the man. "Radical's a pretty strong word for a man who just wants to make sure that his wife is happy, Hugh," he admonished in a slow drawl.

The sound that burst forth from Hugh Tarenton's body had to be a bark of laughter. He pounded Josh on the back.

"I like you, Hawthorne. I do. I'm not sure I like some of your more modern ideas, but I appreciate your gutsiness. Where in hell did you find this guy, Ellen?"

Ellen took a deep breath and pushed her shoulders back. So the fight wasn't over yet. All of her and Josh's work was probably for nothing. It was obvious that Tarenton was amused by her "romance" with Josh, sentimental enough to let his wife offer the family homestead for the wedding, but in the end, he was an old-fashioned man. Jarrod's straight-to-the-bone, old-world approach to life would appeal to him, even if the man didn't have half her qualifications.

"I met Josh a long time ago. A mutual friend," she explained, repeating herself once again as she raised her face to Josh's gaze. He was looking at her with definite concern and she wanted to reach out and touch him, to hug him. If Mr. Tarenton hadn't been standing right there watching, she would have kissed Josh right on those wonderful, magical lips of his—and to hell with what he did to her system. She would have risked all those crazy, rushing sensations that sent sizzling heat through her body whenever she came up against Josh's skin. It would have been worth it, to show him just how much she appreciated what he was trying to do for her. How many men, even in this day and age, would vow to follow their wife's drum rather than their own? Even if the wife was only for pretend?

No one had ever tried to fight her battles for her. She'd always been the one to do things for others, the mother figure in her family, but she was also the kind who got things done simply by doing what needed to be done, not by fighting. Having someone—no, not just someone—having *Josh* battle for *her* rights sent a thrill skittering up Ellen's spine.

"I was lucky enough to meet him through a friend, Mr. Tarenton," she reiterated with a smile. "And you're right, he's a very different kind of man. A generous and caring man," she said, knowing she should tear her gaze away from Josh and face her boss while she was talking to him, but letting herself watch the man who had always mesmerized her for a few seconds longer. "Thank you" was on her lips, but she held it in.

Instead she walked the men back past the machines, depositing the safety gear. She took them down the hall, back into the office. She *thought* she said the appropriate things to Mr. Tarenton as he reentered his office. Right now she wasn't sure. She only was sure that she needed to talk to Josh, to let him know that she was going to repay him someday for all of his efforts that he had offered so selflessly. She just didn't know how.

But taking Josh past Nissa and Karen, an idea began to form. A small something... Not a real feel-good idea or even a good idea, but it was something at least. The women were looking at Josh as if he was a bit of rare roast beef and they were a couple of starving puppies. Karen looked at Josh like...well, the way women had always looked at him. But instead of his usual, sexy teasing grin, Josh simply offered a casual smile, the kind an engaged man would give to a woman he couldn't have.

The knowledge nudged at Ellen, refused to be ignored. If not for this bizarre position she'd placed Josh in, he would be flirting with Nissa. Maybe even Karen, too. It was his way, a part of him. He'd always attracted women, loved being with women. Now he was only with Ellen because he was playing a part.

The thought lodged in her consciousness. She was cramping Josh's style. He had left his clients and all the pleasures of Europe to help her out. He was, in fact, subduing his own personality, denying the man he'd always been.

Ellen felt suddenly selfish. If she hadn't been using his name he wouldn't have come and gotten all tied up in this. But he had come and well, maybe it wasn't a big deal to him, but it meant a lot to her to have him here. Because of that, she owed him. And she always paid her debts.

Smiling apologetically at her friends, Ellen reached for Josh's hand. They needed to talk. The lie of the diamond that graced her ring finger bit into her skin, as if to remind her that it didn't really belong there. She was not Josh's, had never been, and never would be. But still, they were tied for now. It was time to let him know that she'd realized his sacrifice, that she was sorry if she had ever doubted him in the past.

Hanging on tightly to his hand, Ellen moved away from the desks of her colleagues and toward the outer doorway.

"I thought the tour was over," Josh said, folding his fingers over her own so that he was the one doing the hand-holding as he followed her lead.

"Yes." Ellen glanced over her shoulder. She looked into those eyes that had always done such forbidden things to her heart. There was no use in continuing to deny it. At least in admitting her weakness, she could also admit its pointlessness. She could do the right thing.

"The tour *is* over, Josh," she said, "but I wanted to talk to you. Outside is easier."

"Then outside it is," he agreed, slipping his arm around her waist.

He was playing the game again. She knew that. They stepped out the doors.

"I'll have to formally introduce you to Nissa one of these days. Soon. She's the exotic blond woman at the desk nearest to mine," Ellen said softly, her voice a bit breathless as she tried to keep reminding herself that there needed to be some give in this relationship, not only taking. "You'd like her."

Josh's hand tightened a bit at her waist.

"Would I?" He splayed his fingers against her side, his touch sending an ache echoing through her as he made his way to a picnic area on the edge of the parking lot.

Ellen sucked in her breath. She tried to focus on stilling her pounding heartbeat, on ignoring the way Josh's index finger rested just beneath her breast.

"Yes," she managed to say, swallowing hard. "It just occurred to me, she's—well, I guess Nissa's a lot like you."

"Is she?" His voice was a lazy drawl, as he suddenly stopped, turning so that Ellen faced him. His hand framed the small of her back in a seemingly possessive gesture. "And you think this friend of yours and I would suit?" he asked, pulling Ellen even closer so that she was up against his chest as they stood in the center of the parking lot.

Ellen placed her hands palms down on his chest. They felt so right resting there, warmed by his skin even through the layers of his clothing. She should step back, break contact.

"I—I suppose you would. She seems like your type," Ellen agreed reluctantly. "Nissa's beautiful, fun, she likes to laugh and tease. She wanted to know if you had any brothers or uncles or anything."

Josh had moved his other hand to cradle her neck, so that he was up against her, around her, her pretend lover to anyone who cared to look. A tired smile lifted his lips. "And what exactly did you tell her, my serious little lady?"

Ellen sucked in her lower lip and raised her head just a touch so that she could see Josh's dangerous amber eyes. "Nothing," she whispered. "I didn't even know if you had any brothers. I didn't think you did, but I wasn't completely sure."

When he began to chuckle, his chest vibrated, the sound causing an echo she could feel in her fingertips. His skin moved against the pads of her fingers.

"Josh?"

Immediately he dragged her against him, resting his forehead against hers. "I think we'd better spend some serious talking time together, Ellen. I really do. You constantly surprise me. And I apparently am a mystery to you, too. Better not let anyone know that. It might kill our story completely."

Ellen rested her cheek against his chest. For one long minute she drank in his warmth, the scent of his aftershave, his essence—and realized that she was not so very different from Nissa and Karen. If she had a mirror, she'd probably see that same wistful look in her eyes where Josh was concerned. Even the realization that Mr. Tarenton might not be giving her the promotion after all hadn't really hit home as hard as it should. Not yet, anyway. And that was purely due to Josh, she knew. It was the legendary Hawthorne charm that was having this numbing effect on her. She'd seen perfectly intelligent women forget their own names around Josh. Why should she be any different from other women? Why shouldn't she be like Nissa or Karen?

But I'm not Nissa or Karen, Ellen reminded herself. *I'm not my sister or my mother, longing for a man I can't have. I've carved out a different life for myself, a good comfortable life that suits me, one that has its own rewards.*

Dragging in a deep, calming breath, Ellen raised her head. She pushed herself upright. "Thank you for what you said to Mr. Tarenton today," she said. "I should have realized that someone as old-fashioned as he is would balk at transferring a married—or almost married woman—across the country."

"The man is living in a time warp, or so it seems, Ellen," Josh said, gently pushing a stray wisp of hair away from her face. "On the other hand, maybe he's just making excuses to keep his most valuable employee here in his office. I think that might be it, and we'll just have to do our best to change his mind."

Ellen closed her eyes against the feel of Josh's fingers on her scalp, against obeying her own desires.

"Bet you didn't think I'd be this much trouble, did you?"

His chuckle was low, she felt it vibrate through his fingertips. "You never made things easy for me, Ellen."

Her smile smoothed out, dropped away completely. "I didn't, did I? I told Penny that you were the worst kind of womanizer, that you'd break her heart. I don't know why you'd even want to help me."

"Maybe I just wanted to come back and have you frown at me some more. You're pretty when you get that snooty, disapproving look on your face, Ellen. Your eyes rain blue sparks even if you never say a word,'' he whispered, his breath gently lifting the hair on her forehead.

A sigh slipped through Ellen as she stood there, still surrounded by Josh's body. He was warm, big, reassuring and, of course, she shouldn't have expected a serious answer to her question, but that didn't mean she wasn't grateful for his help. It didn't mean she wasn't sorry that she was cramping his style. She hadn't expected this charade to go as far as it had and she'd bet her best briefcase that neither had he. He was being such a rock for her. She wished there was some way she could do a bit of the same for him.

For long seconds she stood there, trying to think of some real impact she could have on Josh's life, some genuine need she could fulfill. But what could she do for a man like that? He had money, he lived life as he wished, he enjoyed women and had plenty of them. Oh, yes, he did, but not lately. Not this week, anyway.

The idea that had crossed her mind earlier surged forth and hit her full in the face. Not much of a big deal, but it was a small something she could handle. In time. She could restore the balance and send Josh on his way a satisfied man. She could fulfill Nissa's fantasies.

A gigantic ''no'' welled up in her heart, but she forced it back. This desire she was feeling for Josh right now was temporary, not real or lasting. This feeling of rightness in his arms was in fact very wrong for a woman like herself. And she wanted very much to do the right thing, the smart thing for everyone.

''Josh.'' Ellen forced herself to find her voice, to lean back in his arms. ''I—I know that I've been less than a good friend in the past, and now it seems I'm doing all the taking, none of the giving. Let me do something for you, too. All right?''

His arms tightened about her, pulling her back to him. He blew out a deep breath, and dropped a kiss on her hair. ''Ellen, you are one pushy little woman. Have I told you that? If not, I *do* know that I've told you I don't need any payback from you, so what exactly is it that you want to do?''

Ellen shifted in his arms, shivering at the sensation of her body moving against his. She forced herself to stop moving. ''Would you—would you like to meet Nissa?''

Silence spread through the air. It lingered.

And then, when he hadn't answered, when the only sound was that of the stillness, as if both of them had stopped breathing, she closed her mind to the brittle bit of pain that was growing within her and plunged on, determined now to set things back on their natural course once all was said and done.

''I know you don't actually need my help with your love life.'' She tried a weak chuckle. ''But you've always been a connoisseur of women, and Nissa is, well, I've always suspected that she was very special. I could—I'd *like* to introduce the two of you properly.'' She pushed herself to make her pale offering, the one that was no doubt unnecessary to Josh, but suddenly very necessary to her own sanity.

She reached up, clasped his wrists, and looked straight into his suddenly cool amber eyes. ''I'd like to do that,'' she said again.

He slipped his hands away, cupped her face in his palms.

''Would you, now, Ellen? Would you?'' he whispered as he brought his lips down to hers.

No, she wouldn't. Not at all. Not at all. And yes, oh yes, because seeing him with Nissa might be the only thing that would break this hold he was beginning to have on her.

Josh's lips moved over hers, softly, slowly, coaxing a reluctant response from her. She heard herself moan, couldn't stop herself from melting into him and kissing him back.

But this was one moment in time. Passing desire. This was only the pretend world she had thrust herself into. This wouldn't, couldn't last.

This time would pass, and then everything would change. Josh would have his life back to normal, Nissa would have her night or two of heaven, and *she,* well at least she would always have her memories of stolen kisses that had never belonged to her at all. She would make things right in the end. It was enough. She would not deny herself the enjoyment of this moment now that she knew everything would settle into place when life returned to normal.

Chapter Eight

So Ellen was planning on paying her perceived debt to him by introducing him to another woman, was she? Josh thought, studying the lady who had made the preposterous suggestion.

Her thoughtfulness touched him, troubled him; it ticked him off royally. Ellen was innocent, a stranger to a man's questing touch, he would bet, but even an innocent knew that Nissa Robards's every look said, "Take me to bed." The fact that Ellen was blithely offering him a lover when he'd been running his palms over her own lovely body every chance he could get, burned. He didn't want a string of nights with someone like Nissa who promised to know every trick in the book, who could make most men salivate simply by breathing hard. No, he wanted just one night with a fussy, brainy, far too serious woman who ran from pleasure every chance she got. He wanted a woman who didn't want him in the least and never had. He wanted—

"Ellen, come closer," he murmured in protest, scoop-

ing her solidly up against him. She fit into the cradle of
his thighs like water in a glass.

Josh cupped her head in one hand, his other stroking
slowly down the curve of her slender back, his fingers
coming to rest over the swell of her hip. He curled his
fingers possessively over the enticing flesh that filled his
hand.

She gasped and her breath was a whisper, warm as it
fluttered against his skin. For several seconds he stared
down at her as she lay in his arms, her eyes closed as if
to deny what he was doing to her. Then, slowly, he covered her lips with her own. She was berry sweet, achingly
soft, her bottom lip trembled as he sucked on it.

Groaning, he slipped the tip of his tongue against the
sensitive skin just inside her mouth.

She opened for him.

Desire exploded within his body, knocking out any
sane thought that might have tried to creep in. He
wrapped his arms around Ellen, felt the stiff tips of her
breasts drag against his chest.

Pleasure. She wasn't completely impervious to him,
after all.

But her eyes were still closed, her long lashes beautiful
against her pale skin. Josh gently kissed her eyelids, willing her to open her eyes the way she'd opened her lips
to his caress. He wanted her to look at him as he loved
her, he wanted to stare into those blue, blue eyes as he
lowered her to the ground, held himself on stiff arms and
slid into her depths. He wanted—

A car's engine sounded in the distance, probably there
all along, but suddenly louder, closer.

For ten brief, reckless seconds Josh stood there and
stared down at her, wanting to push the clock back, to

have just a little more time with her. Then he slowly let out his breath, faced reality. A groan escaped him.

And Ellen's eyes did open. She stared up at him, blinking as if waking from a dream.

"Damn, but I shouldn't have done that," he said, lifting her gently away from him, setting her back on her own feet, leaving a generous space between them.

Josh shoved his hand back through his hair, and sucked in deep drafts of air. Hell, if Tarenton didn't already believe they were headed for the altar, he certainly would now. Ellen had nearly found herself lying on her back in the grass only a hundred yards outside Tarenton Toys.

"I shouldn't have let things go so far," he repeated, resting his hands on his thighs for a second, trying to shake the desire that had gotten a hammerlock on him only seconds earlier.

Ellen shook her head. She reached out—a bit tentatively, he thought. "No, don't apologize," she said. "You were only trying to help me."

Josh raised his head and looked her dead in the eye. "That's a hell of a lie, Ellen Rhoades, and even you, novice that you are, know it. Helping you wasn't on my mind at all a minute ago. Helping you out of your clothes *was*."

The word "novice" hung in the air between them. They both knew that he had spent a great deal of his free time helping women out of their clothing and that she was not the type of woman to succumb to that kind of persuasion as a rule.

To his surprise, she didn't act shocked—or even angry. Instead the slightest of smiles slowly lifted her lips.

"Forgive me if I don't beat you over the head with my briefcase, Josh. You look like you wish I would, but frankly, I just can't find it in my heart to be upset with you for that, especially when nothing actually happened. On the contrary, you've always treated me a bit like some sort of sexless little sister. It's somewhat…reassuring to find that I'm not all that different from other women, after all.''

"Like hell you're not, Ellen. Don't you know that you're about as different from other women as a woman can be? You're a rose in a field of dandelions. You know what you want and steer toward it, knocking all the other possibilities by the roadside. I've always admired your determination to reach your goals. And if you think I never recognized your finer points, that I didn't recognize you as a desirable woman from the get go then you must also think I'm one heck of an idiot. Just because you and I are different doesn't mean I can't appreciate your qualities.''

Ellen lifted one shoulder in a gentle shrug. "I guess that sounded a bit like I was fishing for a compliment. I wasn't, though, you know. I just wanted to let you know that I wasn't offended by your touch. I…I enjoyed it, in fact,'' she said, tilting her chin up defiantly while hot color tinted her cheeks.

Josh held back the groan that threatened to escape him only by sheer willpower. He didn't know how in hell he kept himself from pulling her into his arms again. God, she was magnificent, courageous…beautiful in her honesty.

He stared down into her eyes then, managed to wring a smile from his own lips. "And I enjoyed kissing you…tremendously, even if it wasn't the best idea I'd ever had in the world. You and I—'' He held out his hands, palms up.

"Would be foolish to let something like this happen again. I agree,'' Ellen said quietly, wrapping her arms around herself. "This situation we're in, well, it's only natural that two people who have to spend so much time touching each other should begin to—"

"Sizzle every time they get close? Sear the very grass beneath their feet when they brush past each other?"

Ellen swallowed visibly and raised startled eyes to Josh. "I meant that it's only natural that we should be *attracted* to some extent," she said, emphasizing that prissy little word.

Heaven above. Attracted? It wasn't the word Josh would have used. Too tame when what he wanted to do was peel away her clothing and lick his way up her body. When he wanted to feel the weight of her breasts in his hands, feel her hips arch high against his own, hear her breathing quicken as he slid into her silken depths. That wasn't mere *attraction,* that was—

Insanity.

She was right. It was best to keep this damn thing as low-key as possible, to accept the fact that they were going to be in physical contact now and then and they were just going to have to deal with their *attraction* and ignore it as much as they could.

Josh shook his head and slid one restless hand back through his hair. "It's only natural," he agreed. "And only smart to recognize a weakness when it rears its ugly head. I'll do my best to control my wayward impulses where your beautiful little body is concerned from now on," he promised.

"Me, too," Ellen agreed.

He could almost see her setting her shoulders, arming her internal defenses. Ellen was going to go at this the way she went at everything: with determination and the absolute will to succeed. He would have smiled—if he hadn't felt so much like bellowing with frustration. But he would ignore that frustration, sit in a bathtub filled with ice cubes if he had to. He hadn't come here, after all, to seduce Ellen Rhoades.

"Come on, I'll walk you back to the office. And Ellen?" he said as he waited for her to step in line beside him.

"What, Josh?" She looked up at him.

He grinned back. "Do me a favor. Don't bother introducing me to your friend. I'm sure she's a lovely lady, but—"

"But you don't need help getting dates," she said dryly, smiling and shrugging a bit.

"But I *prefer* to choose my own dates." He shook his head. "Besides, I thought we'd agreed that there were no debts to pay."

"I know, but—"

"But nothing, Ellen," Josh said, refusing to budge when she began to walk toward the building. "You think I'm getting nothing out of this, you're wrong. Dead wrong.

"And I don't mean the thrill of sliding my hands over your lovely skin," he said when her cheeks began to pinken. "Although admittedly that's a sweet little bonus I hadn't anticipated. But what I meant, Ellen, was that it makes me feel good to be able to help you. Very good."

"Josh, you're an attorney. You—"

"Spend my days advising people who already have a great deal of money on ways they can legally make more money. And that's fine. I happen to be very good at it, but it's not the same as being personally involved in seeing a wrong righted. That's what this time with you is. Very gratifying, very satisfying. Like going to the movies as a kid and cheering for the good guys. So it's really you who's giving something to me, you know. Besides,

Ellen, it makes my blood bubble to think that your boss would pass you over for a promotion just because he's still living in the days of peasants and kings. Don't you get angry enough to want to storm his doors? The man can't be so blind as to be truly unaware of your worth.''

Ellen blew out a breath. "Of course I get frustrated. I don't think it's immodest to admit that I know I'm good at what I do. Dennis Jarrod is good, I'm not taking anything away from him, but I *do* have better qualifications as well as more experience. I *am* the logical choice for this promotion, so yes, it's upsetting to have to twiddle my thumbs, to see my chance slipping away. But—I don't know, Josh. Hugh Tarenton is a man of very strong opinions. I've worked for him for years, I've had plenty of time to learn his ways. He likes to reach his own conclusions, not have them pushed at him. Do you really think, knowing what you do of me, that I'd set out to do something as outrageous as setting up this pretense without good cause? This is not my usual style. It's not even your usual style. Don't you think I know that? So, yes, I'm frustrated—and I'm also immensely beholden to you for entering into this so gamely. You can understand why I feel that way, can't you?''

Shrugging, he reached out to take her hands in his own, then shoved his fingertips into his back pockets. More physical contact was probably not a great idea at the moment. "As I said earlier," he finally replied, "don't underestimate the value of what *you're* doing for *me*.''

Ellen stood there staring at him for a second, silent. Then a smile raised one corner of her lips and she shook her head. "Okay, I won't, but I do think that maybe I underestimated *you*, Josh. A man who agrees to go on tours of factories, put up with my friends whispering every time he's around, who fields nosy questions from almost everyone I know, who gives up his time to take me to parties…'' She held out her hands as if she didn't know what to say.

''And skating,'' he added, ducking his head to make direct eye contact with her.

''And…skating?'' she asked, with a frown.

''Definitely skating. We need some downtime, some time to let loose and refresh ourselves. Besides, I promised we'd act like an engaged couple, didn't I? Do you want people to think that I never take my future wife out to have a good time? Do you want people to think all you do is work, that you don't have time to spend with the man you've offered your heart and body to?''

His teasing tone did a bit to chase away the slightly incredulous and anxious look in Ellen's eyes, but not completely.

''Skating?'' she repeated. ''As in roller skating?''

''In-lines,'' he agreed. ''As in music with a lot of rhythm. Moving side by side. Dancing on wheels. It'll be fun.''

She'd never been skating, he could just bet on it, looking at the determined look on her face. She was gearing herself up for it, talking herself into it.

''It'll be fun,'' she agreed. ''Just as soon as you teach me how, Josh. I'm embarrassed to say that I never had a lot of time to learn stuff like that when I was younger.''

Josh suddenly wished he'd known Ellen when she was younger. He would have made sure that she'd had a chance to learn how to skate.

''I won't let you fall—too much,'' he agreed. ''I'll pick you up when you do.''

''And you won't laugh?'' Ellen laughed at herself then. ''Because I can guarantee you I'm going to fall.''

''Ellen,'' he drawled, ending with a chuckle of his

own. "Of course I'll laugh—and so will you. We're doing this for fun. I'm planning to laugh a lot. Even if we spend a lot of time rolling around on the floor together."

His comment and the image it conjured up put an end to both their laughter. Maybe skating and all the nearness it required hadn't been all that wise a suggestion.

"Penny always liked to skate," Ellen offered suddenly. "She only lives about an hour away."

Josh nodded, slowly. "You're right. Maybe she'd like to come. And...your sister. How is she today? I meant to ask earlier. We could make it a party—if you'd like."

Ellen raised sad eyes to him. "I don't know if Lynn would be willing. Thank you for asking, but she's not herself right now. Her husband—ex-husband," she said, correcting herself, "really hurt her. She doesn't feel much like socializing right now."

Ellen's woeful tone, the way she linked her fingers together tightly, the memory of her sister, almost just a kid really, sent fingers of anger slipping through Josh's consciousness. Memories awakened, of his father making excuses, to him, to the current woman packing her bags to leave. He'd treated women like conveniences, hurt them time and time again, put them aside because he didn't have what it took to love back.

Josh couldn't help himself then. He touched her wrist, turned her palm over, stroked his fingers down and linked them with her own, holding tight.

"I've known a few women who've been in situations similar to your sister's. It takes a long time for the hurt to stop. Sometimes it helps just to get out, to act normal when nothing at all feels like it will ever be right or normal again. Or so I've been told," he said.

Nodding, Ellen kept her hand linked with his as they walked back, stopped outside the office.

"I'll ask her," she promised. "But I'm still not sure that she'll come."

Josh twisted his lips in a grim smile. "Tell her that we need her as a chaperone. Explain to her how embarrassing it would be if I forgot myself and made mad, passionate love to you on the skating rink floor. This is a job we're asking her to do. She has a service to perform. She's needed."

Ellen rolled her eyes at his teasing tone.

The gratification of seeing the worried look flee her face was worth the frustrating ache of desire that rose within him at his words. And truth to tell, he wasn't exactly lying. With Lynn and possibly Penny there, he wouldn't risk losing touch with reality; he wouldn't risk doing anything foolish.

"I'll tell her that we *really* want her to come," Ellen said, changing Josh's words. "I'll tell her that I need her to teach me the ropes. Lynn learned how to skate, to fly like she had wings when she was barely able to toddle around."

"And what were you doing while your sister was learning to skate?"

"Oh…I don't know. I had other things to do."

Like tying her sister's skates; picking Lynn up, taking care of her little brothers; working, always working, as she always had, he'd wager. Well, not tonight. Tonight Ellen would get to be the kid she'd never been. Tonight she would have wings, she would throw back her head and laugh with delight.

And he would take a mental snapshot of her…so that he would remember this night once their time together was gone and they both took their rightful places in the world.

* * *

Josh had finally made it back to his hotel room and was getting ready to change when he got the message from the front desk.

Dear Josh,
When I called Rome and heard you'd come back to the States without letting me know, I was ready to pin you up by your ears, but I love you and your secretary tells me that there's some possibility that you're engaged, so I guess it's okay that you decided to steal a little private time without contacting your favorite stepmother. I would have waited for you to come in, but my plane is leaving soon. Expect me in Midland at 6:30. Sorry, but I just can't wait any longer to meet my future stepdaughter-in-law.
                                         Love, Alice

P.S. I'm happy if you've finally found a woman smart enough to win you over.

A smile stole over Josh's face, even as he shook his head. Alice. His father had wedded her, bedded her, and deserted her when Josh had been only twelve. And during the short two years she and his father had been married, the two of them, woman and child, had become close. She'd seen the lonely kid inside the flippant boy, the one who'd longed for the unreachable fairy-tale ending. He'd seen the very real, if rejected, love she'd had for his father. Together, they'd stood up for each other, made laughter when there shouldn't have been any. They'd banded together all these years, long after she found a truly good man, long after he'd become a success by life's easy standards. Though she was only fifteen years his senior, she was the mother he'd never known.

Alice was family, and though he'd tried for obvious reasons to keep her out of this situation, it didn't surprise Josh that she had made her way in anyway. She counseled the divorced, helped locate deadbeat dads. Finding him and learning of his engagement would have posed no challenge. And he couldn't be too sorry that she was coming. Alice was a natural mother, even if she'd never had children of her own. She would not be another taker in Ellen's life. For Josh wasn't about to allow any more takers into Ellen's life—not even himself, no matter what needs she called up in him.

The man made her feel like a kid at her first fireworks display, Ellen decided when Josh finally showed up that evening. She was always watching, waiting for him to appear. Like the great bursts of color that lit up a summer night's sky, Josh always made her shiver just by breathing, being alive, even when she'd promised herself to behave like an adult.

It was very important that she behave like an adult. So why, when she saw his car rolling down the street, did she lock her door and start making her way down the hall?

Because I've completely lost my judgment, she realized. *Because I don't want him to think that I don't appreciate the opportunity to learn how to skate at age twenty-nine,* she amended, not really sure which was the correct answer.

Stepping out the door of the building onto the walkway, Ellen gasped as Josh reached her, wrapped his arms about her and whirled her around in a big circle so that her back was to the car.

"Hello, lovely Ellen. I have a surprise for you," he said as he nuzzled her neck.

Ellen drank in air, fought the urge to let her head fall back to give Josh better access.

"A surprise?" she asked, barely able to get the two words out.

"Mmm-hmm, only—"

"Yes?"

"Only I'm not sure whether you're going to like it," he said, setting her on her feet and grinning down at her. "In fact, I'm afraid you're going to be very angry with me."

Cold panic settled in her body like frost on morning grass. Was he leaving town then? Had this game played out for him? She couldn't ask the question, could only look up at him and wait.

"Is your sister coming?" he asked, instead of ending the suspense.

"Yes. Penny's got a date, but Lynn agreed to come after I begged her." Ellen continued to wait for Josh to drop the bomb.

"Good. I'm glad she's joining us. Then this will *really* be a family event," Josh whispered, leaning to kiss her lips briefly, then kiss them again. "My stepmother is in the car," he said, his mouth still touching hers.

"What?" Ellen straightened. She pulled her hands away from Josh's chest where they'd come to rest like homing pigeons. "I'm standing here while you're kissing my throat—"

"And your lips. And this absolutely delicious spot here," he agreed, grinning broadly as he brushed a finger against the sensitive underside of her jaw. He leaned forward as if to press his lips to the spot where his fingers had rested only seconds before.

Ellen swallowed hard and stepped back. "Josh, your

stepmother is watching,'' she said, pressing hot palms to her face.

"And Alice is loving every minute, Ellen, I promise. She's always wanted to see me in this position. Engaged, I mean," he added, when Ellen looked up at him suddenly.

"I hate deceiving her," he confessed with a frown, "but Alice wouldn't thank me for the truth. Not yet. She has what she's always called 'the cursed face of a too-honest woman.' Her eyes won't let her lie, and she'd feel ten kinds of guilt if she was the one to reveal your secret. Besides, Alice loves a good game and she craves justice. She'll be happy if this charade helps you win out over Tarenton in the end.

"Come on. She wants to meet you, sweetheart," he confided. "And I confess I want you to meet her, too. You're both pretty special ladies. Besides, Alice has been where your Lynn is now, Ellen. She knows what that kind of pain is like. My father treated her every bit as badly as your sister's husband is treating her. Maybe she can be of some help to Lynn, make her feel less stranded, less alone. Alice is very good at what she does. At least I can assure you that she won't do anything that will hurt."

Ellen sighed and placed her hands back where they had been. That he should be thinking of Lynn's welfare while they were all setting off on this farce of an evening amazed her.

"She sounds like someone I'd like to meet," she whispered, turning in his arms to face the car. "I just wish I didn't have to make her acquaintance wearing wheels that are flying out from under me."

Josh's laugh rang out into the night, reaching the secret places in Ellen's heart. "Don't worry, you're one hell of a lady no matter what you're wearing. Come on, let's go meet Alice and let her spend a few hours telling us how many grandchildren she wants us to give her. And Ellen,'' he said, stilling her briefly by slipping his hand around her waist.

She looked up, tilting her head back to study those amber eyes that had turned dark and serious.

''I know this is uncomfortable. I'm sorry to spring this on you, but I promise things will work out. We're in this together, and you have my word I won't do anything to embarrass or hurt you. This evening will be fine.''

He'd been right, Ellen acknowledged as she slowly made her way around the rink on a ''ladies only'' number. The evening had been more than fine.

Alice was a dear, an attractive fiftyish woman who was very sharp and who obviously loved Josh to distraction. She was, as Josh said, hugging her, a mother-of-the-universe type and within ten minutes of meeting Lynn, the older woman had coaxed a near-smile from the younger woman who obviously needed a smile badly. Josh's natural inclination to tease had set everyone at ease. He'd made a special point of drawing Lynn into the conversation. It was good for her sister to see that all men weren't like Richard.

But that wasn't the only reason why the evening was so fine, Ellen knew. Spinning around the room with Josh's arm guiding her, his hand resting on her waist, was heady stuff. Being the object of his attentions was having the same effect on her that it would have on any woman. Locked into the scenario she'd created herself, she could no longer retreat to the safety of distance where Josh was concerned. And being close to him was as devastating as she'd always known it would be.

She was, Ellen couldn't help but acknowledge, becoming her mother, her sister. She was falling hard for a man she had no business falling for. And sooner or later she was going to hit the ground much harder than any time she had tonight.

"You're doing just fine, Ellen." The low female voice sounded close to Ellen's side, and she took her eyes off her skates just long enough to see that it was Alice who had skated up behind her. The woman had obviously made her way around a rink before, Ellen acknowledged, studying the way Alice effortlessly handled the crossovers on the turns.

"I'm getting by," Ellen admitted with a laugh. "I can't believe Josh actually talked me into this. Learning to skate at age twenty-nine is a little different, I'm sure, from learning at age nine."

The older woman laughed, turning so that she was skating backward, facing Ellen. "Maybe, but you can learn a lot at any age. Like now, for instance. I'm learning that maybe I was wrong about Josh."

A slight warning thrum began to build in Ellen's chest. "Wrong? In what way?"

"Well…" Alice cocked her head as she kept skating. "I love that guy. He was the only person I had to love for a long time, and though he was just ten when I married his father, he was already wise beyond his years. He tried to protect me from Les's infidelities. When I was so filled with hurt that I was almost incapable of functioning, Josh tried to make me feel better. He'd leave little things on my pillow and try to make me think that Les had left them. A flower, a pretty stone. I think that part of it was that he didn't want me to go away and leave him in that big old house with only his father for company. But part of it was also because we were so much alike. Les didn't have much use for either of us at that time.

"Anyway, I do love Josh," she continued, "but he's always seemed to be burdened with the same Hawthorne Curse that plagued Les. He's never really found a woman he could love and stay with. I'm glad he finally has. I can see that he really cares for you."

The thrumming in Ellen's chest grew stronger. Her stomach rolled over. Tears formed behind her eyes imagining Josh as a child, trying to help a grown woman, trying to find some sort of love for himself. Josh who had needed a friend, a mother. Josh, who still hadn't found a woman he could love.

The beat of the music, the sound of skates on hardwood filled Ellen's ears. She swallowed hard.

"And you've kept in touch with him all these years?" she managed to say.

Alice nodded. "Josh was best man for my Dan when I remarried ten years ago. We always manage to touch base a few times a year. Usually I'm the first person he calls when he gets back from a trip, but…I don't mind giving up my position as most valuable person in his life as long as I know you really care about him."

She did. She really did care about him, Ellen thought, nodding at Alice. And sooner or later she was going to suffer the type of pain that Lynn and Alice knew, but for her, it would be different. She would have her eyes open; she would have brought her broken heart upon herself. She should never have named Josh as her fiancé when she first conceived of the idea.

But she had, Ellen acknowledged as the song ended and she saw Josh, tall and proud, making his way across the floor to her side.

She had, and pain or no, she could not be completely sorry.

"Miss me?" Josh teased, as he slid his hand to her waist, cupping the dip between her rib cage and hip.

"I was counting every millisecond until you returned," Ellen responded dramatically, rolling her eyes. Josh would never know how much wholly unacceptable truth was shrouded by her teasing comment.

"She's got just the right touch of fire in her. She'll make you a good wife. You two enjoy each other," Alice called with a smile as she turned and began to skate off in Lynn's direction.

For two or three seconds, Ellen leaned against Josh's hand, just enjoying his nearness. Then she tilted her head to look up at him.

"Will she be very hurt, do you think?"

Josh blew out a breath and slid his hand up higher as he pulled her closer. "Maybe not about the deception. Alice will definitely understand. But about the fact that I'm not getting married? She'll be disappointed, but... she's fair, and she's tough. She'll take a deep breath and go on."

And so would *she*, Ellen thought. When Josh left, life would seem tame. She would be disappointed. No, more than disappointed, but that didn't bear thinking of. The important thing to remember was that she had always known that this was a fairy tale, and a fairy tale couldn't break a woman's heart, not when it had never been real in the first place. She was a real woman. She would go on after she'd said her goodbyes to Josh Hawthorne...and only in dreams would she see dark amber, teasing eyes laughing down at her. Only at night would she remember her pretend lover who had come and brought unexpected light and laughter to her life.

When she was in Phoenix, none of that would matter, anyway. She would have her life as she'd always envisioned it, and she would be grateful to Josh, send him a Christmas card once a year. She would listen to Penny tell tales of his latest escapade...and smile at her memories. She would not cry; she would never cry...not over a fantasy lover. It just wasn't going to happen.

Taking a deep breath, Ellen raised her chin and looked way up at Josh.

"Teach me to skate backward?" she asked.

Without another word, Josh spun her in his arms, caught her, his hands framing her rib cage just beneath her breasts. And suddenly she was facing him, her feet wobbly, held up only by the strength of his arms.

Her hair blew backward over her shoulders, tickling his chest. She looked up into his eyes.

"Ellen," he drawled in a low, smooth voice. "You're getting dangerously adventurous, aren't you?"

She smiled and shook her head. "Not really so adventurous. After all, you promised me that you wouldn't let me fall—too often."

He returned her smile, and dragged her closer...so close that only his skill kept their skates from colliding. "And I won't let you fall. I promise I won't let you get hurt, Ellen."

But of course, he was wrong. She would get hurt in the end. Ellen knew that. And he was also right about the other. She *was* getting adventurous.

Because nothing was going to stop her from enjoying this short time she had with Josh. No matter the consequences or the inevitable outcome, she was going to take this pretend time they had together and grab it with both hands.

She would worry the *next* day about how she could

speed things along, how she could convince Mr. Tarenton to choose *her* for the position opening up in Phoenix. And tomorrow she would face the fact that whether she got the promotion or Dennis Jarrod did, her time with Josh was rapidly coming to a close.

Chapter Nine

Ellen stretched, then rose up in her bed and lifted her hands to the sunshine-coated ceiling. Blinking, she breathed in deeply, taking in the fresh air that drifted in her window. Last night had been wonderful, she remembered. Last night she'd gone to sleep and dreamed achingly passionate dreams. Remember-for-a-lifetime dreams.

But this wasn't last night any longer. This was today, and the bright light of truth was upon her.

It was time to get back to her life. Her *real* life.

Sliding from the bed, Ellen rested bare toes on the floor and began to plan her day.

Today she would submerge herself in work, pile it on and up. Make decisions, make progress, make a difference. She would leave absolutely no doubt in Hugh Tarenton's mind as to her abilities. She would keep her nose buried in work—which would be easy. Josh was spending the day with his stepmother.

Ellen nearly groaned as she forced the man out of her

thoughts, forced herself to take a cool shower, dragged on a suit that was more than usually boxy. Black pin-stripes, white blouse with a tight white collar and a string tie. She armed herself with sensible black flats, and picked up her briefcase.

She was set for business. She was all ready to work that man right out of her system. By the time Mr. Tarenton either gave her the promotion or passed her over for Dennis Jarrod, she wouldn't really even mind that Josh was slipping back out of her life.

Yeah, right. And amber wasn't really the color of Josh's eyes.

"Oh, Ellen, are you in trouble," she said, dropping her briefcase back on the table.

It was going to take a lot of work to avoid thinking about Josh today. She didn't even want to guess at how much effort it would take to evict him from her dreams completely.

Josh punched in the number for Tarenton Toys, the one that would give him instant access to Ellen's desk. He didn't even ask himself why his hands were shaking. He'd grown used to that lately. Just the sound of her voice did that to him. Hell, just the *thought* of her being less than ten minutes away made him start to ache.

"Tarenton Toys. May I help you?" Ellen's soft, musical voice came over the line.

It was the standard greeting used by thousands of businesses. Why then, did it seem so suggestive now?

Because he was losing touch with reality, getting in deeper than deep, because he was totally frustrated by the need to do the right thing by Ellen and keep his grubby paws to himself.

"Hi, sunshine," he finally said. "Working hard?"

He could almost imagine the delicate touch of pink inching its way up her throat. God, he loved the fact that she lost it so easily when he talked to her.

"Josh." She drawled out his name sweetly, slowly. She was killing him, absolutely killing him, and they'd hardly said a thing.

"It's pretty busy," she admitted.

Uh-oh, not good news. He didn't need to add to the pressure she already had at work by making her get backed up on things.

"I won't keep you, then," he promised. "I just wanted to let you know that Alice sends her love. She's going shopping for a present for Dan this afternoon, I think she's taking Lynn out for dinner and I thought you and I—"

"I'm working late tonight, Josh. I can't get away. There's just so much to do."

Her tone was breathy, rushed, not even close to the calm, cool woman he'd seen handling megaproblems at work before. Something was bothering her, something big.

"All right," he said slowly. "I'll meet you later then. We need to talk."

They did, he realized as she hesitated, then finally agreed to see him, as he hung up the phone. He wanted to find out what was making her so skittish. He wanted to do something about it if he could. He wanted to give her, *get* her anything she wanted on earth—and soon. It had to be soon. This couldn't go on much longer.

Every time they were together he was on the verge of spontaneous combustion. He'd break both his wrists before he would do anything to hurt her, but it was so damned hard to keep away from her. He looked for excuses, any excuses to talk to her, look at her, be near her, touch her.

And she wasn't immune to him, either. She *didn't* want to feel the desire that raged between them, that licked at him constantly. It wasn't in her plans. He had to respect that. He had to do his best to bring this whole thing to closure. She was stressed, and so was he—and there was always the imminent danger of disaster.

He didn't know what in hell Tarenton was waiting for, whether the man was playing a game or simply being selfish, but Josh knew that the man realized Ellen's worth and was ignoring it. Josh had clients, friends, his own damned companies for crying out loud, who would pay big bucks to headhunters to scope out someone with Ellen's people skills. Ten, no, a thousand times he'd considered offering her a position with one of his firms or asking a friend to find one for her, but she wouldn't want that. *This* was her proving ground, this had become more than a job. She'd started here, she'd played by Tarenton's unfair rules and this was where she wanted her worth to be validated. Josh understood that; he respected Ellen for her tenacity.

But he wished the game would end soon. Coming here to help Ellen had been both the best and the worst decision of his life.

"It's going to take a long time to forget this woman, Hawthorne," he said to the empty telephone line. It was what every woman his father had ever left had told him: Getting over a relationship took time.

"*Relationship, hell,*" he muttered. This had been more like a nonrelationship, more like *avoiding* a relationship. Still, he was going to have to recover from whatever it was, and it *was* going to take a heck of a long time. The sooner he got started the better.

It would be best to get started, to move on and out as soon as possible, but…he couldn't desert Ellen now. She still needed him—and so he couldn't start forgetting her, either. Damn Hugh Tarenton's hide for making everyone wait.

It was time to jump out of the plane without a parachute. Way past time to take the next step.

"Hey man, good to see you."

"Hi, Josh."

"Hello there, Mr. Hawthorne."

Josh made his way through the maze of desks at Tarenton Toys, waving and nodding as he went. He was beginning to feel like a part of this place. No, that wasn't exactly right. He was *beginning* to feel as if he really was Ellen's fiancé.

"Josh, are you looking for Ellen?" Nissa walked up beside him as he neared Ellen's desk. "I think she's over on the other side of the offices right now. Some little girl in the day-care center fell on her nose and her mother's in a meeting right now."

"Day-care center?"

"Yeah, it was Ellen's idea a couple of years ago. A bit modern for this company, but even Mr. Tarenton heartily endorsed it. You know, the family thing and all."

Yeah, he knew about the family thing. It was why he was here.

Injustice. Josh had a sudden, nagging need to check into his own backyard. He hoped he didn't have any Ellen Rhoadeses working in his own companies, people who were having to play silly games to accommodate outdated rules.

Nodding to Nissa, Josh begged instructions and started off toward the east side of the building. But as he neared

Hugh Tarenton's office, the man stepped outside. He was carrying a jacket and a briefcase.

"Been waiting for you, Hawthorne. Thought I'd hit you with an idea before I cleared out for the day."

Josh waited, tilting his head.

"Play golf, Hawthorne?"

Rarely. He was all right, but it wasn't his sport of choice. No matter. Admitting that would end this conversation. That wasn't in Josh's plans.

"I play," he agreed.

"Good. Good. I'm getting together with a couple of the executives at Holiday Hills tomorrow. Make it a foursome?"

"Sounds good to me." That statement wasn't exactly true. Spending his Saturday on a golf course with Hugh Tarenton when he'd planned to suggest something to Ellen didn't really suit him. But he had to take opportunities as they came. He needed to get to know the enemy—and a golf course was as good a place as any.

"Good. Good," Tarenton croaked. "We've got a one o'clock tee time, then. You know the place?"

He did. He'd passed it on his way into town from the airport. What he didn't know was why Hugh Tarenton was asking him out for a jaunt on the golf course with his right-hand men. Not that the Hawthornes weren't well-situated themselves, not that they weren't considered high-powered players in certain parts of the country, but not around here. Here he was just Ellen's fiancé. He hadn't sent his résumé on ahead of him.

"I'll be there," Josh assured Tarenton as the man gave him a farewell salute and headed for the door.

Interesting. It would be damned interesting to find out what Tarenton wanted to talk about. He'd know soon enough, but first there was Ellen, and the prospect of a few minutes with her was a lot more enticing than a few hours with Hugh Tarenton.

Josh stopped and asked directions from an administrative assistant clearing off her own desk for the night. She pointed to a glass door leading to a brightly painted hallway. He had barely moved out into the hallway when he saw Ellen walking toward him, accompanied by a tall blond woman. Ellen was carrying a small, sleeping child.

"I think she'll be fine, Marge," Ellen said, soothing her hand over the little girl's back. "She was more scared than hurt. Please, don't go home and blame yourself for being in a meeting. You came as quickly as you could, and Lindsay was fine, anyway, once she realized that you were just across the hall. She asked for her teddy bear and a story and went to sleep right away." And so saying, Ellen placed the slumbering child in her mother's arms.

The other woman smiled and shifted her child to a comfortable position. "Thanks for being there for her, Ellen. She adores you. You're such a natural mother. I really hope you and Josh have loads of babies."

Ellen had already noticed him coming toward her. Josh could tell it in the way she suddenly straightened, the way her eyes widened. With Marge's words, she turned her head to the side, avoiding his gaze. She ignored the woman's remarks.

"I'll make sure everything's in order at your station, Marge," Ellen promised. "Lindsay's exhausted and I'll bet you're more than a little tired after that three-hour marathon of a meeting yourself. Tell her I'll bring the book tomorrow. Someone must have lost or walked away with the center's copy of *Love You Forever* and it's one of her favorites. Fortunately I know most of the words by heart. My nieces and nephews like it, too."

Marge called out her thanks and her goodbyes, gathered her child closer and moved on down the hall.

"You're a very lucky man. I hope you know that," she told Josh, smiling at him as she passed him in the hall.

He did. Of course he did know how lucky he was to have had the chance to get to know Ellen Rhoades. But right now he didn't feel lucky. He felt…restless, hungry…and angry at himself for feeling that way. Josh brushed his emotions to the side. Giving in to them would only put more pressure on Ellen right now when she'd already had a long day.

"Crisis?" he asked, coming closer.

She shook her head. "No, not really. Lindsay had a bloody nose. My youngest brother used to get them all the time and it's always so frightening for a child. With all that blood, they think they're dying and who can really blame them? She was just a scared little girl who needed some simple first aid and lots of hugs."

"Which you provided. Aren't there people to staff the center?"

Ellen crossed her arms defiantly. She lifted her chin and looked up at him. Uh-oh, he'd hit a nerve. Hadn't Nissa said that Ellen started this center?

"Of course there are people who staff the center. The best available. But sometimes there's a special situation, and this was one of them. Lindsay wanted her mother, and no one else would do. So…"

"So you stepped in and solved the problem."

"I did what anyone with a heart would do."

"Only ten times better," he said, raising one brow as he smiled.

Ellen opened her mouth as if to offer another retort,

then let out a long sigh and returned his smile. "Thank you—I think," she said. "I'm sorry if I was snippy."

"Don't be sorry. It's only natural that you'd be defensive. I hear you started this center. What other miracles have you worked lately? Today?"

She wrinkled her nose at him. "I'll have you know that I only work miracles once a month on Tuesdays. Today I mostly worked my way through a mountain of paper."

"And dried a little girl's tears."

Ellen shrugged. She pushed through the door leading into the main office, heading for her desk. "I hope you don't mind if we don't leave right away. I really *do* need to get a few more things done before I go," she said.

Yeah. Like cleaning up someone else's desk, he thought, remembering her words to Marge. He stifled the statement. No point in irritating Ellen again, not when he only wanted to help her.

"No problem. I stopped by the nearest law library and picked up some reading material. I'll work alongside of you, if you don't mind." He held out the book on labor law that he'd checked out earlier in the day.

Sighing, Ellen looked at the book and frowned. "I'm not sure I'm ready to go that route yet," she admitted.

"I know, but I seem to have developed an interest in the subject lately. Don't mind me," he ordered as he settled into a nearby chair. Still, Josh couldn't help seeing that there were several stacks of paper, and several notes on Ellen's desk with other people's names on them.

He sat there for long seconds, trying to pretend to read. Then, "Is all that work yours?" he finally asked, unable to hold the note of censure back.

"Josh," she chastised. "I *do* know my job. If one of the people who work under me needs a little assistance in understanding something or if they get overloaded, I step in. It's what I do. It's the way I am. I'm a worker bee, all right?''

''You're everyone else's rock to lean on,'' he insisted.

That was it. He'd ticked her off royally now, Josh conceded. She came out from behind that desk, stepped right up to his chair, leaned over him—close. Real close.

He wanted to reach out, touch her, tumble her down across his lap. Instead he tightened his grip on the book.

''Josh, I appreciate your concern, but that's how part of this whole problem started, with someone else trying to decide what was best for me. And that won't work. I have to make my own choices. I have to be my own person,'' she insisted.

She was right. Like it or not, she did make her own choices, and had gotten along just fine before he came along. She'd probably manage superbly after he was gone.

That didn't stop him from worrying about her, from wondering who would watch out for her, who would make her laugh and slow down now and then once he was gone.

Josh wiped an impatient hand across his brow. He let out an impatient breath. She *was* her own woman, she was an adult, and she would not want him hanging around for the rest of her life worrying about her.

Even if he wanted to.

''You're right,'' he said, smiling up into her eyes. ''I'm being overbearing and judgmental. Must be the strain of knowing that I'm playing golf with the big guy tomorrow.''

Ellen straightened to a stand. She took a deep, shuddering breath, crossed her arms and began to pace.

''You're playing golf with Mr. Tarenton. Why?''

Josh managed not to grin. "Because he invited me along? Because it seems like a good opportunity to let him talk about his plans."

Whirling, Ellen paced back the other way. She stopped beside Josh again. Her hands were fluttering like shadow puppets. "It'll be fine," he assured her, catching her hands in his own, stroking his thumbs lightly across her palms.

She shivered, but instead of pulling away she leaned closer, her dark hair swinging close to his lips. "Josh, you don't have to do this for me," she reasoned. "It could be—unpleasant."

Chuckling, he did the unthinkable then. He pulled her down on his lap, felt her sweet bottom settle across his thighs. "Well, he'll probably win the game if he's halfway decent, that's for sure. I'm usually lucky to break ninety, but—I'm not the kind to cry over a loss. Even if my opponent taunts me."

She bunched her brows, trying to look down her nose sternly. "You know that's not what I mean. He might ask you personal questions. I don't want you to be put in an uncomfortable position."

Licking her lower lip, Ellen leaned forward anxiously. Josh caught a strand of her hair between his fingers, and caressed it. She might be the caretaker of the rest of the world, but no way was he going to let her start worrying about him right now. He wasn't going to take from her the way everyone else always had. *He* was here to help *her,* because he wanted to, needed to, not the other way around. "I don't think even Tarenton would be so nosy as to intrude into our bedroom, Ellen." His lips were close to her cheek, his words a whisper.

She shook her head, and he felt her shudder against

him. "No, of course he wouldn't do that, but there are so many things you don't know about me."

Josh smiled then, and let go of her hand to slip his fingers beneath her chin. He turned her to face him.

"Ellen Elizabeth Rhoades, born August 19th. One sister, Lynn. Three brothers, Robert, Jeremy and Douglas, two nieces by Jeremy, two nephews by Robert. You hold a degree in marketing and have worked at Tarenton Toys for seven years. Your favorite foods are chicken divan and toffee crunch ice cream. You're beautiful, loving, and the most capable employee Hugh Tarenton has ever hired."

Ellen looked deep into Josh's eyes then. She tried to control the trembling that overtook her. How had she ever thought that this man was just a carefree gamester, a man with no substance? No wonder women loved him. How could anyone help it? And how could she not feel guilty about the position she'd put him in with her thoughtless pretense?

"And what about you, Josh?" she asked, feeling his fingers brush the sensitive skin of her throat as she spoke. "You play golf—a little. You advise rich clients on their business prospects, you're interested in labor law, you lend your services to those who need justice, you're very popular with the ladies," she said, tilting her head in a salute. "You have a stepmother who knows just what a wonderful human being you are, and a father who's been married a number of times. I've always thought you must have led a charmed life, but Alice said that wasn't so. Tell me, Josh. I want to know."

She stared into his eyes then, and saw the pain of years gone by. She saw that he looked at her as if he wanted her—but that wasn't surprising. He was, after all, a man who loved women. It hurt to admit that she wasn't unique, but right now she wasn't looking for compliments for herself. She wanted to, needed to know, who Josh was.

"Looking for another someone to help, Ellen?" he said, shifting so that she wasn't so close. "It's not necessary, you know, even though Alice was right. I *am* my father's only child, and it's true that he *wasn't* much of a husband or a father. I don't think he really had it in him to care about someone deeply—at least not for very long. In fact he wasn't even around much except when he thought some future bride needed impressing. Then he'd call me downstairs and ask me a few pertinent questions about my grades, that kind of thing. But, Ellen," Josh said softly, still staring into her eyes. "I'm not going to let you dwell on that. It's long gone, I *did* have a mother in Alice, and you're not going to take me on as your next pet project. As you said, I'm an adult now. The past doesn't matter, all right?"

He was wrong. That was all she could think as she studied his face, longing to stroke her fingers up through his dark, silken hair. The past *did* matter. He had needed love and not gotten it. Maybe that was why he steered clear of that emotion now. And then again, maybe he was right. She was delving into his personal business when he hadn't given her the right.

"All right," she said on a sigh, sliding one hand beneath his jaw and stroking her thumb over the dark shadows of his cheek. "I'll go along with your wishes. The past is past. You're an adult."

She took a deep breath and peeped at him from beneath lowered lashes. He was grinning at her, nearly laughing.

"Ellen," he said, in that low, sexy voice of his. "You look very put out with me. I'm sorry that you weren't around when I was a boy. Maybe we could have comforted each other, but if you keep shifting around on my lap like that, you're going to find out just how much of an adult I am. And this time I'm not going to apologize.''

Ellen sat up straighter then, and felt the evidence of Josh's adulthood growing. He groaned, bent and kissed her fingers as he suddenly lifted her off his lap.

''To work,'' he ordered. ''That will give you something to do and me something to think about besides taking you to bed when I know that's impossible.''

She stood there, looking down at him, not wanting to leave yet. ''Josh, I—''

He put down the book that he still hadn't looked at. ''I'm a man, not a monk. I'm trying to do the right thing, and keep my hands off of you like I agreed to. So go back to work, please. Give me a chance to get my mind off your beautiful body. And then, when you've worked your way through that mountain of paper, when a couple of hours have passed and I'm ready to think with my brain and not...other parts of my anatomy again, then we'll talk. We'll plan the next step in our strategy.''

It was a sensible solution, and ordinarily Ellen would have flown into the stack of papers on her desk. She should have been running from him and his honest remarks. Josh was everything she'd never allow herself, all the things she couldn't have and couldn't risk. He was a danger to her sanity and her future and she ought to be doing all she could to ignore him. And work—work had always been her refuge, it had always taken her mind off whatever was bothering her. But today all she could think of was Josh sitting a few feet away, Josh wanting to take her to bed. All she had to do was sit right here and work. All she had to do was walk right over there and ask him to make love to her.

Then it would be over. Then he'd have her out of his system like all the other women he'd ever made love to, and everything would be back to normal.

Ellen closed her eyes, opened them again and grabbed the first paper off the stack. She wanted Josh. It was all she could do to sit still and keep from begging him to kiss her, to touch her, but—she didn't want everything to be over yet. No. If he was going to forget her—and of course, he was—then she didn't want it to be now. Not just yet. Every intelligent cell in her body told her to end things now. Every emotional cell told her to hang on just a little longer.

So she closed off her thoughts, her desires. And she worked. Somehow, someway, she worked, she got a few things done. But then—

"Josh, what is our next step going to be? What is it you have in mind?" she asked, staring up into amber eyes that were already turned her way.

He held her gaze as he lowered his book to the table. He rose to his feet and walked to her side, never letting her turn away from him.

"It's a simple decision, really." His voice was quiet in the still, darkened office. Shadows surrounded them, cocooning them in privacy.

Ellen lifted her face to Josh's, studied the hard angle of his jaw, the banked fires in his eyes, unwilling and unable to drop her gaze as she waited for him to continue.

"All we have to do is answer one question, Ellen." He leaned closer, planted his palms on her desk, staring down into her upturned face.

"And what is the question, Josh?" she asked, wishing he weren't so close. No, wishing he were really much nearer.

"The question is—when are we getting married, Ellen?"

Chapter Ten

Ellen was looking at him as if he'd just asked her to do the unthinkable. As if he'd just asked her to take her heart out and do a tap dance on it.

He shook his head and grimaced. ''What I meant to say, Ellen, is that I think we need to call Hugh Tarenton's bluff. The man hasn't budged. He needs a nudge—or maybe a heck of a kick in the rear. It's possible that my reputation has preceded me, and he isn't going to take the bait until he's sure we're really going through with this.''

But of course they weren't really going through with anything. Ellen was *not* marrying him; she had looked positively shocked when he'd asked her. It had been stupid to phrase his question in that way. Hadn't he promised himself that he wouldn't be like the rest of the world, that he wouldn't make demands of her the way everyone else did? Between her sister, her boss and all the other people who were always pushing their needs before hers, it was a wonder that Ellen could see straight. He refused to become just another user in her life.

She studied him carefully, not answering for a long time.

"I—I hadn't really wanted things to go this far," she finally said, blowing out a breath and looking away.

He tucked one finger beneath her chin. "Didn't I tell you the man was a manipulator, that you'd have to take the plunge?"

She hesitated, then nodded, feeling his touch slide against her skin. "You did, but—"

"I promised to stand by you, too," he reminded her.

She brought her head up at that. "I wasn't doubting you," she said angrily. "That doesn't mean I want to drag you in deeper."

"And if I'm in anyway? Because it's my own choice and I want you to win? I want every woman here to win when you finally take the step up, when you eventually break off the 'engagement' and show Hugh Tarenton that his empire won't tumble down just because a capable, talented and extremely 'unmarried' woman is in a high position of authority. I want to hear about that, Ellen. I do."

Ellen swallowed, and kept staring into Josh's intense golden brown eyes. She knew he meant every word. He'd come to her, offered his help, he was committed. She no longer knew what she wanted for herself, not really, but she knew darn well that she wanted to give Josh Hawthorne whatever it was he wanted and needed.

Sucking in her lip, dragging in deep breaths of air, she nodded quickly. "All right then, we'll set the date."

Josh's stance relaxed slightly when she agreed to the plan. But his eyes were still narrowed with concern, and Ellen was sure that his only anxiety was for her. From the moment he'd shown up, he'd had her best interests at heart.

A slight light began to glow within her as she realized that Josh *had* considered her more than a challenge, not just another adventure. He was a genuinely good and caring man. Alice's words last night had just confirmed what she had already known.

And now he was still worrying about her. He'd tried countless times to get her to loosen up, lighten up, smile. He'd always been doing that—and to be honest, he'd always succeeded, even when she'd been younger.

"Just tell me the date. If you like you can make the announcement on the golf course," she agreed, sliding her hand out toward where his own rested on her desk. "Maybe that will keep him from quizzing you—or do you think it will make your golf outing even more unpleasant?"

"I'm not worried about unpleasant, Ellen. I'm worried about you getting the credit you deserve."

She shook her head, smiled. "Then don't worry. I'm sure Mr. Tarenton will be waltzing me around the room once he hears the good news."

It was probably true, but it wasn't the main thing Ellen was thinking about now. She was thinking that she wanted to give Josh Hawthorne some of his own medicine. Good medicine, that is. This time *she* wanted to spend some time making *him* smile. And it wouldn't be because she was one of those people who took on everyone else's troubles, either. Oh sure, she'd spent a lot of time looking out for other people in her life; mostly out of love, and yes, sometimes out of simple duty, but this was different. She didn't just want to make Josh smile; she wanted to share his smiles, his teasing laughter. She wanted him to know for sure that she wouldn't regret this time they'd spent together, whatever the outcome. Even if her silly plan backfired, even if it didn't work, she didn't regret setting all of this in motion.

Uh-uh, not one bit, Ellen thought with a smile, standing to face Josh.

"Want to come puppy hunting with me tomorrow morning?" she asked, purposely making her voice low and sultry, trying to imitate the low, teasing tone that Josh was so good at.

"Puppy hunting?" He blinked hard and straightened to his full height. Good, she'd startled him, she'd chased that look of concern right off of his face.

"You know." She leaned closer. "The humane society. Woof-woof, little furry creatures that cuddle up to their owners and lick their faces."

He gave her one of those lopsided grins, the kind that kicked her heart right over and made it flip around.

"I *do* know what a puppy is, Ellen. What I want to be told, though, is *why* are we puppy hunting?"

She held out her hands and shrugged. "Lynn."

"Ah."

"Yes, ah. Actually, Alice suggested it last night. It seemed like a good idea. Lynn was always good with animals. The responsibility of a dog would give her something to think about besides her own problems right now. I thought I'd just test the waters tomorrow, see if there were any cute little guys that might make her forget Richard ever existed. If we find a likely candidate, then I'll broach the subject with her. I thought maybe you'd like to come, too. For fun."

"Fun?"

"Adventure. You know, the thrill of a challenge."

"A trip to the humane society is that dangerous, is it?"

She crossed her arms, held her grin and her ground.

"You just never know, Josh. There's always the danger that you'll come home with something you never planned on. I thought you might come along to help restrain me."

"Oh, Ellen, you wicked woman," he said, leaning near her. "How could any man resist a challenge like that?"

"I thought you'd like the idea," she said with a smile. "Come on, let's go eat. Pizza today, puppies tomorrow."

And a few more hours with Josh. She meant to make his last remembrances of her happy ones. When he left here, she didn't want him worrying about her. She didn't want him to spend the rest of his life popping back in to check on her. She didn't want to spend the rest of her life waiting for those brief moments when he was around—as her mother had waited for her father. She definitely didn't want to sit around wondering if she could get him to come back and stay for good—as her sister was doing with Richard. When Josh left she wanted the ending to be razor sharp and complete with the knowledge that they would never meet again. Then she could begin to be strong.

But for now there was laughter—and there was still Josh.

He'd never had a dog. She could tell it by the way he handled the puppies as if they were overgrown eggshells, and by the absolute look of wonder on his face.

"So what do you think? Do you see any puppies that might make Lynn a good companion?" she asked.

Josh gave a low whistle as he contemplated the matter. He held a roly-poly puppy that looked like a mix of shepherd and lab, one ear standing at attention, one flopping over. As Josh rubbed the little guy right behind the floppy ear, the puppy let out a pitifully small rumble of approval. He licked Josh's hand.

Holding him higher, Josh stared his newfound friend straight in the eye. "I don't know," he said, laughing, "but even though I've never met Richard, I'd bet this little sport would be a hell of a lot more loving and loyal."

Ellen reached over and gently stroked the puppy's nose. He closed his eyes, whimpering his delight. "Frankly, a hammerhead shark would probably be more loyal than Richard ever was." She studied the earnestly enthusiastic puppy. "He's certainly huggable, isn't he? But he *will* get to be big, Josh. Right now, he's a bundle of fluff, but little bundles grow."

"Good guard dog, then," he protested. "Your sister's alone. She could use a big dog." He continued to stroke the dog's fur, gently sinking his fingertips into the soft stuff as the puppy pushed closer, licking at Josh's hand madly.

"Maybe, but...her apartment's sort of small, Josh. I don't think the landlord would let her keep such a humongous pet."

With a curt nod, Josh carefully lowered the puppy back into his cage, signaling to the attendant who'd allowed them to look. "You're right, of course. Sorry, buddy," he said, giving the little guy a gentle tap on the behind, turning immediately away as the gate banged shut. But Ellen saw that his eyes weren't as cool as his voice.

She could see a much younger Josh saying goodbye to yet another stepmom who had come into his life, promising motherhood, then leaving again. She could easily imagine the eager look in a young boy's eyes when the father who never talked to him, demanded his attention, even if it was simply to impress a potential bride. He had been forced to close off his heart again and again—and now he'd learned to do it automatically.

Ellen looked at Josh, grown now, a stunning example of a man, a warm and caring man who still had never found anyone he wanted to stay with for a lifetime. Maybe he never would. Because he hadn't met anyone whom he could love, or simply because he'd never allowed himself to stick around long enough to get too attached? She didn't know, and maybe the reason didn't matter. All that really mattered was that Josh would probably always be a man moving from one relationship to the next, for whatever reason. She should remember that, take warning.

She stared at the shaking little creature looking at Josh with longing in his eyes—and knew instant kinship. She would have liked for Josh to have that puppy, but she was aware that, like Lynn, Josh's life-style wasn't suitable for raising a potential monster of a dog. Neither was her own. No. Definitely not. It *wasn't,* she reasoned, forcing herself to walk away and keep walking.

"Here," Josh said, pointing to a feisty miniature terrier. "Look at this little guy. Lots of grit, tenacious. He'll stick by her through anything," he predicted, as the skinny little fellow rose to all fours and pointed his nose through the silvery bars, trembling with indignation and growling slightly as if to warn off any intruders, big or small.

"He's so fierce, Josh," she agreed, laughing. "I don't think he knows that he's no threat to anything bigger than a mouse."

"Doesn't matter. He's got confidence. He'll be a good example to his mistress," Josh predicted. "And just let Richard try to get in and steal away with that wedding ring or anything else he's decided he wants back. This little guy would probably chew the shoestrings off him."

The thought of Richard struggling to get out the door

with a tiny terrier attached to his foot made Ellen smile. "Maybe you're right. This could be the one. I'll bring Lynn back tomorrow, and hope her baby tiger is still available," she agreed.

Slowly she and Josh looked around, then began to make their way to the door, but Ellen couldn't keep from looking back over her shoulder at the tiny shepherd-and-lab that had caught Josh's attention. The poor little guy had his head cocked to one side, his almost-not-there-yet tail was wagging slowly, his eyes entreating as they made their way past. She also couldn't keep noticing the way Josh's back stiffened at the puppy's small, mewling cries. He knew this was something he couldn't have. He couldn't help this puppy, not when he spent so much time flying around the world, never being around in one place long.

"He'll be all right," she said, knowing that her words might not be true.

"Hey, how could he not be all right? How could he be passed over?" Josh agreed.

But Ellen knew that it could happen easily. He would one day be a veritable monster of a dog, not the type that everyone would want.

She let out a long sigh, and wandered back to the puppy. "You know, I really *was* planning on buying a house when I moved to Phoenix. I never intended to spend my whole life living in an apartment," she reasoned. "And while I'm getting everything organized, Buddy here could stay with my brother for a short while. Douglas has a yard the size of a small village and a heart ten times larger. His home would be a perfect place to train a dog. I thought I might visit him, take a vacation before I made the move anyway."

Josh studied her closely, his eyes dark and intent.

"Helping someone out again?" he asked.

She shrugged. "Look at him. How can I resist?"

The little dog's tail was wagging harder as the cage was opened once again. Josh leaned over and patted the squirming bundle of overactive puppy.

Keeping his eyes trained on the furry little ball that he lowered to the floor, Josh went down on one knee before his newfound friend. He looked up at Ellen.

"Did I really once accuse you of being too logical?" he asked over the little animal's body. "I must have been out of my mind. You're the lady who goes looking for a dog for her sister and comes away with one for herself, too. And not just any dog, but one who promises to be able to give pony rides around the neighborhood. A bit of a rash decision, Ellen. One might even say dangerous," he said with a smile, cocking his head and motioning as the puppy puddled on the floor.

"No, it's not a rash decision," she said, planting her hands on her hips. "If I'm moving to a new town, I'll need a friend." And now that she *had* made up her mind, she knew that she was right, that maybe this outing had actually been just as much for her as for Lynn. Maybe the timing was a bit off, considering the fact that she had yet to make the move that would provide her with the space she'd need for a growing dog, but her choice was entirely reasonable, once all was said and done.

Because she, who had always loved solitude, was going to know loneliness once Josh was gone. Because this puppy would always remind her of one special day, one special man, and because she needed someone who could take all the love she had in her heart. The bond with this small creature was already made, it was set in cement— and it would be a strong and lasting one.

She would give this puppy all the affection she could

not allow herself to give the man. She could save this small creature and comfort herself in the bargain. It would have to be enough.

"You want to borrow my Big Bertha, Hawthorne?" Hugh Tarenton offered, holding out the club. "A man your size needs a big driver, big son of a gun."

"Thanks, but I'm fine."

What a damned lie, Josh thought as he lined his shot up, and took his chances with a Holiday Hills rental club. He was anything but fine, had spent his whole night rolling around in the sheets, churning the bed into a mess of mixed-up blankets, sheets and pillows.

He could still see Ellen leaning down to rub her nose against the soft fur of that puppy, he could just imagine her wrestling with the leash of the barn-size dog the animal would someday become. Not that he doubted the creature would be as loving and gentle as a dog could be, given Ellen's tutelage. But still, he suspected she'd saved the fuzzy little thing more for Josh Hawthorne's sake than her own. She was still looking out for the welfare of the world, only now *he* was the recipient of all that charity.

And charity was not what he had ever wanted from the woman.

Josh took a long, arcing swing and sent his ball sailing a good two hundred yards right into a wooded area.

As if he cared.

"Got your mind somewhere else, Hawthorne?"

Josh raised his chin, and looked toward the blustering man who had the privilege of being Ellen's boss.

"As a matter of fact, I do, Hugh. Ellen finally agreed to let me set a date," he said, sticking to the truth, knowing that Ellen would feel better if he didn't make the lie bigger than it already was.

To his surprise, the older man stepped up beside him. Tarenton put a meaty but gentle arm around his shoulder.

"I'm glad, son. I'm truly glad," Hugh Tarenton said. "Ellen's always been a bit skittish about relationships, you know. I have to admit that I've been a bit worried that she might bolt before this thing was done. Nothing against you...or her, either, you understand. No, Ellen's always been straight as an arrow. She'd work herself sick if we didn't have weekends every five days, but that's always been the problem. Her job has always come before her life. Not that it's bad to be a hard worker. I admire her. Really do."

Josh studied the man and saw the sincerity radiating from his eyes. Once again he wondered if Hugh Tarenton would ever let Ellen go. Maybe he just wanted to keep her close by. Maybe naming a wedding date wasn't going to do a whit of good.

He wanted to ask the man why he hadn't already promoted Ellen. He wanted to demand that she be given her due this minute, but that wasn't his right. Ellen had started this all on her own; she had to choose how to finish it. Indeed, if the world was as it should be, she would have already marched up to this man and demanded her rights. She'd earned them, and she should never have had to resort to extremes to climb one step up the ladder. Tarenton understood her value. Surely the man wouldn't have done something foolish if she'd simply made some reasonable demands.

"I'm glad you see her worth, Hugh," Josh said. "May I relay the compliment?"

"Hell, yes. She already knows she's a credit to the company, but you tell her, anyway. And Hawthorne?"

"Yes?" Josh leaned on the cart and waited for Hugh to get in. He waited for the other members of the party to move ahead.

"I've got something else to tell you, Josh, and this is something I *don't* want Ellen to know."

He was halfway tempted to tell the truth, that he wasn't keeping any secrets from Ellen, but that would have only shut Tarenton up. Instead he waited expectantly, watching the man open and shut his hands in anticipation.

Tarenton turned in the cart, and smiled a slow smile. "If everything goes as it should, I'll have an announcement to make at your wedding. Big announcement. One might even say a life-changing announcement. You understand what I'm talking about?"

Josh stared dead into Tarenton's eyes.

Hugh began to whistle the wedding march.

Did he understand? Josh almost wanted to laugh. He would have if he hadn't been so totally ticked. *Oh, yeah, he got it. Of course he did.*

Hugh Tarenton was still dangling that promotion like a wriggling worm in front of a starving fish. Because what Hugh Tarenton wanted was a married executive, and he wasn't taking any chances that Ellen might get her promotion until she was handcuffed to a husband for life.

The man was going to force her hand, Josh thought, gripping the golf club tighter—anything to keep his hands from clenching into fists.

What the heck was he going to tell Ellen? How was he going to be able to help her now?

Chapter Eleven

Josh sat at the table on the balcony outside Ellen's kitchen, his hands framing a big mug of coffee, wondering how in hell to drop the bomb that would crush her dreams, that would signal the end of his relationship with her. A sunny Sunday morning should never begin this way, he thought, staring at the brilliant blue that blanketed the world spread out below him. Bad news should only come on rainy days so that it wasn't such a kick in the head.

She looked over at him from behind her own mug and tipped it up to her lips. He could see the hesitancy in her eyes. She knew that he wasn't here to bring her the morning paper.

"Bad news?" she asked, carefully lowering the mug to the glass tabletop. She spread her fingers flat against its hardness as if to brace herself for what he had to say.

Josh stared straight into those silver-blue eyes that could make him shake with wanting, the ones that were probably reading right through to his soul this very min-

ute. He was losing his ability to tell pretty lies around
Ellen—or maybe he'd never been able to do that with
her. Maybe that was part of what made her so special.
She didn't want the lies. It was for damn sure she'd want
the truth straight up right now.

"Tarenton thinks you're the world's greatest employee. He knows he's found something unique in you,
Ellen. You need to take advantage of that, stand up and
claim what is rightfully yours. It's no sin to recite your
strengths to an employer when you're only stating the
obvious."

She closed her eyes, and attempted a small smile.
"Things went that badly, did they?"

Watching her, Josh wanted to swear. There she was
again, putting up that brave front, controlling herself for
his sake. Well, no way was that going to happen this
time. She was a strong woman. She managed the troops
down at the plant with firmness and good humor because
it was her job and Ellen Rhoades always gave her all to
whatever task she took on. But now it was time she gave
her all to herself, long past time she took a stand *for*
herself and to heck with everyone else.

"He's planning on giving you the promotion as a wedding present," Josh said, rising, not caring that he was
towering over her—or that anyone roaming the sidewalks
could see them. "He's prepared to play hardball, Ellen,
to force your back to the wall. Are you going to let him
get away with that?"

She tipped her head back, her dark hair catching on
the fabric of her white blouse. She looked as fresh as the
day, her eyes clearer than the sky, but her skin was still
rosy from sleep, he had gotten here that early, Josh reminded himself. He shouldn't be springing something
like this on her before she was really awake, but he'd

spent the midnight hours pounding out his frustration on his too-hard mattress, and he had turned toward Ellen's door at first light. If she was going to get bad news, he wanted to be the one to tell her, so that he could hold her if she needed it, comfort her if she'd let him.

Ellen stared at him, breathing out great, sighing puffs of air. Then she shook her head and smiled gently as she reached out one hand to touch the tense muscles in his forearm.

"You know, you make me feel powerful when I've only ever felt capable in the past. I've always followed the rules, Josh. I've done the right things and been given the rewards as a consequence. Even at Tarenton, I worked my way to where I am by simply doing what was required and reaping the automatic benefits of a job well done. Only lately..." She let her hand drop to her side.

"The rules no longer apply, do they?" he asked, lowering his voice, coming around behind her chair and resting his hands on her shoulders.

"No," she admitted with a small laugh, "but even then, I thought I could simply try to go along and play the game I was supposed to play. It was silly, wasn't it, thinking I could pretend my way to where I wanted to be?"

Josh stroked one finger up the side of her neck beneath the silk of her hair. He smiled at the sensation of her skin beneath his, smiled at her wistful words. "Maybe ill-advised," he agreed. "But who would have thought Tarenton would have been so stubborn?"

She shrugged, sending soft strands of hair cascading over his hands. "I suppose he knows me better than I thought he did. This town isn't small, but it isn't giant-size. Take two women with horrid mistakes of marriages and a third related woman who's always avoided matrimony as a result. What's the likelihood she's going to change her mind out of the blue?''

Ellen's words sank in, right into Josh's heart. ''I'd say those chances are next to none. Could be we underestimated Hugh's perceptive abilities.''

Nodding, Ellen tilted her head against Josh's hands. She sighed. ''You were right, you know. I should have taken my chances the straightforward way. I shouldn't have tried to stay inside the safe black lines the way I always have.''

''Still time,'' he soothed. ''I'd love to see it, sweetheart. And I'd bet a year's worth of legal fees that he's going to go for it. The man is pigheaded, he's an unfair old bully, he's totally unwilling to change with the times, but…''

She looked up at him, waiting for him to finish.

''But he's not stupid, sweetheart. He would never be so foolish as to let someone like you get away, just because you refused to dance to his tune.''

Who would be so foolish as to let her get away? Josh thought, staring down at her beautiful upturned face, that long stretch of white neck he longed to press his lips to.

No man in his right mind would send this woman walking. And if Tarenton *did* turn out to have stuffed animals for brains, then Josh Hawthorne would be waiting. He'd catch her if she fell, he himself would love and care for her until she got back on her feet.

That last thought shot through him, strong and selfish. He knew darn well in that moment that to live his life loving Ellen was what *he* wanted, not what would make her happy. Still, if she needed him, he would be there for her.

Ellen took a deep breath. She smiled a brilliant smile up at Josh. ''I don't know if you're right, Josh, but I can certainly see how you've wormed your way into women's hearts all these years. You make me feel as if I'm invincible. Right now I can't think of one good reason in the world why I shouldn't march right in there to Mr. Tarenton's office, hand him a list of my qualifications and tell him I want that job in Phoenix, married or not.''

She stood, grasped the collar of his shirt and pulled him closer as she rose up on her toes. ''What is it about you, Josh, that makes a woman feel as if she could work miracles?''

Nose to nose, she faced him, then dropped a light kiss on his lips. ''Thank you for talking me into doing things the right way, clean and quick and honest,'' she said, releasing her butterfly grip on him. ''And for standing by me all this time.''

He smiled down at her, shaking his head. ''No. Thank you. For the adventure,'' he said, letting them both make one more attempt at pretense.

Her smile was brilliant, it cut him right through to the heart. ''It *was* an adventure, wasn't it?'' she whispered. ''I don't think I've ever had a real adventure before in my life.''

''Well, sweetheart,'' he said, his voice low and husky as he tumbled her forward and brought his lips a breath away from hers. ''This was a doozy, wasn't it? The best ever.''

And as his mouth crushed hers, tasting her, as he spread his thighs and brought her close into the lee of his body, closing off the space between her skin and his, he remembered her comment about working miracles. She was right, he knew that. She *was* a woman who could work miracles, but then he was pretty damn sure that she'd always been that, that he'd always been drawn to

her, like it or not. And in the end, she'd worked the
greatest miracle of all. He was in love with her, heart and
soul, and this love was the deep-down forever-and-al-
ways kind, the kind that would haunt him all the nights
of all his years. It was just too damn bad that he'd finally
found what he was looking for with a woman he could
never have.

Strange what a jolt of reality could do to a person's
perspective, Ellen thought as she prepared herself for battle the next day. All this time she'd thought that what
she wanted was to be in a position where she could be
totally independent and free, completely on her own for
once—and she'd been wrong. Total independence was a
fallacy. For the truth was that she'd never be completely
free of Josh, she'd always care for him, want him, miss
him. And maybe that had always been the case. Maybe
that was why she'd run so hard, why she'd never allowed
herself to see him as he truly was all those years ago.
Because she had wanted to be free of him.

Self-preservation was a powerful force, Ellen knew
that. Josh liked her, he desired her, he might even care
for her just a little, the same way his father had cared for
all those women he'd married, but…trying to hold on to
Josh would be like trying to empty a lake with a sieve.
Ill-advised, she thought with a smile, remembering his
assessment of her situation.

She'd chosen Josh as her fiancé, because…she'd loved
him in her dreams for a long time. That was the truth,
the reality she could no longer hide from.

Time to face reality, Ellen, she thought. Time to face
the hopelessness of those old dreams, too, and to get on
with a different kind of reality.

Ellen took a long, soothing breath, and forced herself

up from behind her desk. Reality was here, like it or not, and she was ready—almost. Because she *did* need to face Mr. Tarenton, she did have to try to work the miracle that Josh had assured her was possible. She owed that to every woman in this place, she owed it to Josh for championing her—and she owed it to herself. Her work *was*, after all, what would keep her sane once Josh was gone. Putting off the inevitable was wrong. Waiting would just be a lie. She'd know she was just trying to keep Josh here with her, trying to drink in enough of him to last her a lifetime. And that wasn't fair, to him or to anyone. He'd been right all along. Sometimes a person needed to admit that following the rules didn't work, sometimes the only thing to do was reach out and take a chance.

She closed her eyes, counted to ten, then to twenty. She thought of Josh, of his laugh, his smile, his encouragement. "Okay," she finally said, pushing back her shoulders. "It's show time, Ellen." She brushed her fingers over the photo of Josh, gathered her strength and moved across the room.

Today she would make her demands of Mr. Tarenton, place all her cards, good and bad, on the table. She would do what she should have done long ago—before Josh came and walked away with what was left of her heart.

Marching into Hugh Tarenton's office, she studied him as he looked up at her. He was not a young man, not a slim man, not a man in the best of health, most likely—but he was not to be underestimated. She'd done that already.

"Ellen?" he asked. "You needed something?"

"I do, Mr. Tarenton," she conceded, taking a seat without being asked. "I really do need something. I need your attention for a few minutes."

He threaded his fingers together, leaned forward. Intimidating. Imposing.

She raised her chin.

"Mr. Tarenton, I've worked for you for a good many years. I've been a faithful employee and I've contributed significantly to the success of our division, especially in the last three years."

Tarenton raised one brow. He remained silent.

Ellen felt like she was suffocating, like she wanted to leap from her chair and run. But she thought of Josh, she kept his face in front of her, remembered the pride in his voice when he spoke of her. She stared Hugh Tarenton in the eye.

"I've been a chief force in employee relations here, Mr. Tarenton. I don't think you can deny that. Production has improved substantially since I've been in my current position, and I believe much of that is directly attributable to improved morale. I've worked hard to make every employee aware of his or her own worth, I instituted the plans for the day-care center, I've acted as the go-between for you and those people working in the plant as well as those in the office. I've been attentive to the concerns of both labor and management and have been successful at ironing out many potentially sticky situations. I've negotiated with the hospital to provide day care for our employees' sick children, I helped set up our flexible schedule program so that our employees could mesh their work schedule and their life schedule. I think—no, I *know,* Mr. Tarenton, that I've done a good job for you."

Silence spread out through the office. Hugh Tarenton took a breath, leaned back in his chair, seemingly casual to someone who hadn't seen him take that stance many times before—just when things were getting tense.

"Admitted, Ellen," he said. "Go on."

She leaned forward because she'd seen a hundred employees lean back at this time, unaware that Hugh Tarenton was closing in for a kill.

"The point I'm trying to make, Mr. Tarenton, is that I've been an asset to the company. I *am* an asset. I am the logical choice for the impending promotion, but— you haven't wanted to give it to me, and I'm aware that it's because I'm not married," she concluded.

"Not married *yet*," he said, correcting her.

Ellen's heart began to gallop. All right, cards on the table, she reminded herself. Think of Josh, be confident, take control.

"No, Mr. Tarenton," she finally said, her voice gentle, lower than she would have wished. "Not likely to be married—ever. I never was engaged to Josh. When you began to talk about promoting less experienced and knowledgeable men over me, I took a risk. A mistake, I'll concede. I made up a lie, I made up a fiancé. My fault, not Josh's. He wasn't even aware I was using his name at first," she said quickly when her boss's face began to redden, when eruption was imminent.

He slammed his fist on his desk, he opened his mouth, shut it, opened it again.

"You tried to trick me?"

"I'm an excellent employee, Mr. Tarenton. You'd be hard-pressed to find someone willing to work as hard as I am, but there was one thing I was unwilling to do. Buy my promotion with a marriage license, marry without love in order to impress my supervisor. I'm sorry, Mr. Tarenton," she said then, rising to her feet. "I really should have been honest with you from the start, but you were also wrong. Trying to run people's personal lives, holding their jobs hostage in order to interfere, is no way

to treat those who have been good and faithful employees. And as I said, before, I've become something of an
expert on the subject. Think about that, Mr. Tarenton,
before you take such a stance again.''

Ellen turned toward the door.

''You realize you'll never get that promotion now,
don't you?''

She looked over her shoulder. ''I wouldn't have gotten
it anyway, would I?''

''If you'd just married Hawthorne—''

''That was never an option, Mr. Tarenton. I'm sorry I
led you to believe that it was,'' she said gently.

He stared at her, his eyes hard and unyielding. His
hands were balled into fists.

''I'll have to fire you. Can't have employees lying to
their bosses. There are rules, Ms. Rhoades.''

She nodded. ''I've always lived by them. I know that,
but this was one I couldn't live with. I'm not going to
apologize for that. I won't be begging, either.''

''Good. End as you began, without a fuss. I'd appreciate it if you'd clear your desk as soon as possible. Jarrod's been hinting for a better spot in the office.''

Okay, so that little barb hurt, stung, nearly made her
gasp with pain. Ellen cast one last glance at Hugh Tarenton's tight-lipped expression.

She managed to leave the room with dignity, managed
to quickly grab the few things she wanted from her desk.
With the photo of Josh in one hand, she grabbed her
briefcase and left the offices of Tarenton Toys for the last
time.

Tears rolled down her throat as she thought of all she
had lost, as she realized once and for all what the future
held—or didn't hold. Everything had ended in a big heap

and Josh would be going now. There was absolutely no reason for him to stay any longer.

Josh shoved his tousled hair back from his forehead and headed for the door. Someone, probably housekeeping, was rapping away repeatedly. They wanted in badly. He hadn't allowed even the maid into the room for the past two days. His reasons were suspect, he knew that. He'd worn home the scent of Ellen. He'd taken her essence with him when he went to bed and wrapped his arms around the shapeless hotel pillow that didn't begin to approximate the lady's curvy form. No way did he want that smell of "hotel" to obliterate the tiny hint of Ellen that he had carried here. He would give up all of her, every trace, soon enough. But not just yet.

Closing the open snap on his jeans, not bothering to put on a shirt, Josh reached for the knob. He would send whoever it was packing and tell them to come back some other year. But as he stepped back, pulling the heavy door over the deep blue pile of the carpet, his fingers clenched around the bare brass.

Ellen was standing there, a bulging, totally overstuffed briefcase in one hand, a photo of him in the other. Her long hair clung to her damp face in places, her huge eyes were more silver than blue right now. They were cloudy, misty, swimming in dewy teardrops as she tried to smile and blink the damning evidence of her pain away.

"Hi," she said softly. "May—may I come in?"

She'd never been here since that first night; she wouldn't have come here unless something drastic had happened.

Josh swore beneath his breath, cursing himself, already knowing he had cost her dearly. He'd stolen the things she'd valued most in life: her dignity, her independence, her career.

Taking the briefcase and the photo from her and plopping them, somewhere, anywhere, Josh reached out for her. He drew her into the room, nudging the door shut with his knee. No damn way was he letting go of her now. No way would he try to let her struggle through the rough stuff alone.

"I'm sorry," he whispered, tucking one finger beneath her chin, kissing her damp eyelids closed. "So damn sorry, sweetheart. I should have been there for you, I should never have talked you into mixing it up with that overbearing ba—"

Ellen slipped her fingers over his lips, looked up at him, her hair tossing around her as she shook her head.

"No, don't condemn yourself, Josh. You were right. I *needed* to get everything out in the open, I needed to speak to him alone, to clear the air. I'm *not* sorry about any of that, not at all. Honesty really is the way to go," she said, trying out a small, hiccupy laugh.

Her brave attempt totally slayed him. Banding his arms around her, Josh nudged her chin up, pressed his lips to the underside of her jaw.

"How bad is it?" he asked, whispering his words as he tried to love the pain out of her, tried to make her forget even as he was questioning her. He'd do anything to spare her this interrogation, but damn, he had to know how badly he'd hurt her, how much he'd cost her.

She breathed in deeply, tipped her head back, allowing him greater access. She brushed her fingertips over the bare skin of his chest.

Josh sucked in air as her fingernail grazed his nipple. He slid his hands up the long willowy length of her back.

"I'm out the door," she said at last. "He was pretty steamed. Who could blame him?"

Ellen pulled back slightly, she framed his face with her hands. "It wasn't your fault, Josh. Not mine, either. I don't want you berating yourself."

"Tough. You ought to know by now that I do pretty damn well as I please. You know that, don't you?" He pulled her closer, whispering his words in her ear.

He could feel the shiver trace its way through her body.

"That's what you always claimed," she finally said, her words choked, hushed.

"Then you know when I say that I want you to come with me, I mean it. I'm a wealthy man, Ellen. I want to share that with you, I want to introduce you to people who will cherish everything you are, who'll fight for the honor of having you work for them, who'll offer you everything that Tarenton wouldn't and didn't. Ellen, I want to ask you to—marry me?" he asked, forcing those all too-important words up through his throat, holding his breath even as he held her tightly.

He cupped the back of her head gently, not wanting her to raise her head and see his eyes. If she did, she would know everything. If she did, she would guess at how desperately he wanted her to say yes. And she would give him what he was asking—for his sake, not for her own. He didn't want her to come to him for that reason.

Ellen felt her heart galloping, wondered why it wasn't bursting clear of her body, so desperately was it beating.

She closed her eyes and tried to breathe slowly, to calm herself. Josh had offered her himself, all tied up with silver paper and sparkly ribbon. She ached to reach out and grab the prize, to take what she wanted so badly. Her fingers shook with need and she forced herself to fold them closed—curling them into fists so she couldn't take what wasn't really hers.

He was blaming himself for her pain. He didn't know that her tears had little to do with the loss of a career and everything to do with the loss of a man she'd never know so closely again.

With great effort, she tried to shake her head. He was well-to-do, he could afford a wife, he could link her up with influential businesspeople—and she would be a good wife. She would not embarrass his faith in her business sense, either. She would be a credit to him. It would be so easy to take what he was offering.

Except that she would regret it every day of the rest of her life—even as he would. To love a man to desperation and know that he had offered for her out of pity, to want to give him every inch of her heart and know that it would be too much, that it would smother a man who'd avoided attachments, would be wrong. That one selfish act would cause her more grief than a thousand Hugh Tarentons, a million lost careers.

She loved him too much to let him have his way this time.

"Josh, I—I can't," she finally managed. "It wouldn't work." She gently raised her hand, smoothed it down his dark, stubbled jaw.

"I forgot that you're usually a late riser," she said softly.

But he shook his head, brushing away her concern. He opened his mouth—to protest her rejection of his generous offer, she knew.

She reached for his hand to still him just as a heavy-handed knock nearly sent the door shaking off of its hinges.

"You in there, Ellen?" Hugh Tarenton's voice was dim through the insulated door.

Ellen reached for Josh. She saw the storm rising within him as he stepped in front of her, standing between her and the door when he pulled it back in a sudden, wide arc.

She remembered Alice's words, how Josh had tried to protect his stepmother and a warm glow of gratitude rushed through her. She was glad she'd been allowed this time to know this man...but she wasn't going to let him fight her battles for her anymore.

Sliding under his arm, Ellen faced her ex-supervisor. She could feel the solidity of Josh behind her even if he was no longer touching her, and...it was enough. She tilted her head, stared down Hugh Tarenton.

"I'm on my own time now, Mr. Tarenton," she said, holding her head up proudly. "You no longer have a right to command my time as you please—or to order me around."

A grim smile crept onto Tarenton's lips. "As if I ever did command you," he said. "Whenever you got it into your head that someone needed something, you managed to bring me around, didn't you? Whether I liked it or not? You always knew how to present your damn proposals in a light that I couldn't very well argue with, didn't you?"

Ellen crossed her arms. She leaned back just a fraction of an inch, just for the pleasure of feeling the presence of the man behind her. "Not always," she said.

"All but once," he argued grumpily. "And even then—" Tarenton clammed up, narrowed his eyes. "Hell, even then you convinced me in the end," he conceded, looking like a man who was about to jump into subzero waters. "I made a mistake, I guess," he mumbled. "I shouldn't have tried to force you to live the way I wanted you to."

Blinking, Ellen took a deep breath, leaning back with surprise. She felt Josh's arms on her own, steadying her, making sure she could stand before he let her go.

"I want—" Hugh Tarenton's voice suddenly broke. He cleared his throat. He tried again more softly. "Hell, Ellen Rhoades, you know darn well you're the best person working for all of Tarenton Toys nationwide. I would like for you to come back and take that damned promotion."

She could almost hear "please" at the end of his hesitant speech, but she knew he'd never go that far. He was probably already regretting the indignity of this sudden reversal.

If things were as they should be, she would be jumping up and down, celebrating, grasping the gold ring that was being held out. As it was, she merely felt slightly satisfied. There was definitely an urge to be petty and say "no," to speak the truth and admit that it no longer mattered that much to her, but…there was Nissa and all the other people in the company who valued their freedom. If she took Mr. Tarenton's offer, she could open doors more easily than she could by filing lawsuits. She could grease the hinges, make things happen, make a difference.

"I'll give you my answer in the morning," she finally said, knowing she would take what he was offering. She knew that he knew that, too.

Tarenton nodded slightly, and turned to go.

"And I'll want the promotion guaranteed in writing," she added, stopping him with her words.

He turned, looking back over his shoulder.

"It's not that I don't trust you," she said, holding out her hands palms up, "but..."

Tarenton laughed, that croaky sound she'd learned to know...maybe even like just a little now that things were working out. "But you *know* me," he agreed. "All right, I'll have the agreement drawn up. Be there first thing tomorrow," he said sternly.

She let him have his moment, she waited until the door had clicked shut to turn, to let herself slide her hands up Josh's arms. A small smile lifted her lips.

"Congratulations," he said, with that bigger than life, lady-killing grin of his. He gently bent to kiss her lips, just a light brush, a barely there touch that meant—nothing.

"Josh, I—" She didn't know what to say. Before Mr. Tarenton had arrived, this man, this wonderful man who held her heart, had just offered her marriage. Generously, unselfishly.

He reached out and tapped her nose with one finger. "Hey, don't tell me our engagement's off again?"

She looked up, straight into his eyes. She closed her own, forced herself to keep smiling for a few seconds longer.

"We were never engaged," she reprimanded him, keeping her tone as light and teasing as she could manage.

"No. We were never that," he agreed, his deep, quiet voice seeming to come from a million miles away.

"I guess we just weren't meant to be." She continued the charade, knowing that she had to take it through to the end.

"Never." He played his part just as he always had.

"Where will you go next?" she asked. "Back to Italy?

Rome?'' Taking a deep breath, she managed to pretend a calm she didn't feel.

Josh tilted his head. ''For a short time. To finish up some things. But I have to admit that my plans have changed a bit. It seems my involvement with a lovely and generous lady I know has helped me to see that I can't just sit blithely by and assume that the profits from my business interests mean that all is well in the workplace. I'm sure that lady would agree that a man with a law degree and the responsibility for a number of employees ought to take time to educate himself and get more involved in his own concerns. Particularly in the area of labor relations,'' he added.

Josh smiled into her eyes. He shrugged slightly. ''Can you see me in that light, storming the stuffy bastions of commerce I've ignored for years? Demanding equality for all?''

He looked so darned uncomfortable, unsure of himself. She'd never thought of him that way, seen him like this.

Ellen took one of his hands in her own, that hand that would never touch her again. ''I can see you so clearly,'' she said truthfully. ''Thank you, Josh. For being a hero.''

She brought his hand to her lips.

''Don't.'' He bit the word out. ''Don't call me a hero.''

But he was. He would always be that to her, just as he always had been.

Ellen swallowed hard, knowing the tears were close. She had to leave. Right here. Right now.

''I—I guess this is goodbye then,'' she managed to say.

''Again,'' he said. ''Goodbye again.'' And as she stood there, knowing she should flee but afraid the blur of tears would blind her to any escape route, Josh slid his arms around her once more.

He was going to kiss her. In privacy this time.

His lips came down on her own. Slowly he captured her mouth. She drank ''goodbye'' from his lips—just before she ran for the door.

Chapter Twelve

There had never been a longer day. Ellen was sure of it. And now the coming night threatened to be even more interminable: lonelier. She crept from her bed and slipped out onto the balcony in only her long white nightgown.

Clouds crowded the sky, hiding the moon, but she didn't need the light to know which direction Josh's hotel lay. She could feel his presence. At least it seemed that way. If he'd already caught a plane out, she'd know—wouldn't she?

"Josh," she whispered, as if he were still standing beside her, not setting out on a journey half a world away from her own.

Maybe she felt that way because his face was still imprinted on her soul. In those last seconds they'd spent together, with her eyes on his as he drew her close, she'd thought she'd seen a flicker, a faint touch of light. For half a heartbeat, she'd almost thought she'd recognized—love.

But of course that was what she'd wanted to see. It hadn't been real.

Taking a deep breath, Ellen slid her hand along the rail. She turned it palm up, as if to draw Josh back to her. A futile gesture. He was here—but he was already facing a new direction. She'd lived with that thought all day.

She'd lived with another thought, too.

He'd changed her life.

Raising her head, Ellen let the wind lift her hair; she breathed in deeply of the night. Josh *had* changed her, because all her life she'd been afraid to even think of what others considered the ultimate happiness. She'd run from marriage and love because she'd lived the damage done to those left vulnerable by their need for others. She'd witnessed the failures of those who'd loved, lost, but couldn't seem to move on.

But Josh had come to her, he'd believed in her—completely. He'd taken up her cause because he had faith in her abilities and had made her aware of herself in a way she'd never been aware. What's more, he'd helped her realize that she wasn't just Delia Rhoades's daughter, Lynn Baron's sister. She was an individual, with her own flaws and fine points. She was Ellen, always and only Ellen, and her family's mistakes need not be her own.

He'd made her want to venture far away from her safe little nest, to admit that she'd never see the clouds that painted the mountaintop if she didn't attempt the climb. She'd never know the promise of happiness if she didn't hold out her empty hands and ask for them to be filled.

And yet she'd let him walk away; she hadn't taken when he'd willingly offered to give.

Grasping the iron railing tightly she leaned out. She stared at the lights of the town where somewhere, Josh lay sleeping—without her. The breeze buffeted her, but when she swayed, it was with the force of her own emotions.

"Oh, Ellen," she said, sighing deeply. *That hadn't been love in his eyes.* She'd been wrong.

But what if she hadn't been wrong? What if Josh did care?

And even if he didn't, what if she'd missed the chance to tell him that *she* did?

Time was slipping away.

All she had to do was close her eyes—and let the ground drop out from beneath her. All she needed to do was be honest with Josh, to tell him what was in her heart before she lost her chance.

Because?

Wrapping her arms around herself, Ellen raised her chin high. She turned to the tiny shimmer of moon that glowed so faintly behind the clouds, and she nodded to the night.

Because when the dawn came and he left, she wanted him to know that somewhere there was someone other than Alice, who knew him and valued him and wanted his happiness above all else. She had to reveal that to him at least.

Even if she couldn't imagine how she would get the words out. Even if she risked his pity. She would face him—and dare a new adventure.

The thought brought a warm smile to Ellen's lips, a glow way down deep in her heart. Wasn't that one of the things that she loved about the man, that he'd brought fun and excitement and a sense of adventure into her life? Hadn't he dared her, convinced her to venture out on the high wire before?

"He had," she whispered. Oh, yes, he had.

But that time there had only been a career at stake. This time it was her heart.

Then this time she would risk even that, Ellen thought as she slipped back into the house. She closed her mind to every doubt, to every practical thought, every warning that buzzed through her brain as she picked up the phone and began to dial.

Josh was sitting on the edge of the bed, a sheet tangled around his hips, trying to convince himself that sleep would be a safe refuge from the thoughts of Ellen that had been chasing him all day, when the low humming ring of the phone clipped the quiet in half.

He let it ring. There was only one person he was interested in talking to, and she'd already slipped out of his life hours ago. Ellen had practically stumbled in her hurry to escape his arms when he'd kissed her that last time. No way would she be contacting him for a repeat performance.

"Damn," Josh muttered, falling back against the headboard as the phone rang for the fourth time. He knew if he picked the darn thing up that he wouldn't be able to deal with the disappointment. He'd probably put his fist through the wall. Instead Josh trained his gaze on the pebbly hotel ceiling. He concentrated on watching the pale glow from the hotel sign outside that crept through the small crack in the curtains.

It was Alice on the phone—or it was his secretary, wondering again what time his flight was coming in. Hell, maybe it was even his father, or Hugh Tarenton calling to spit out his opinions about idiotic men who didn't know a good thing when it was standing right next to them.

Wrong, Josh thought, clenching his fist, breathing back

the anxiety that clutched at him as the phone rang for the tenth time. He knew a good thing. He *wanted* a good thing. Right now his need for Ellen flowed through him like a swelling rush of deep, dark water. It flooded him, clouded his vision, his mind, and definitely his heart. He would have walked through anything, done anything to get to her, to help her, just to stare at her in the distance.

But that call wasn't her and if he picked it up and confirmed that, it was going to kill him. The ache was going to rise up and choke him, there was no way he would be capable of speech. There was no point in even picking up the receiver.

Still, the ringing went on. Thirteen, fourteen, fifteen, sixteen.

Josh grabbed the receiver. He started to slam it down again.

"Josh?"

The sound was distant, small, the receiver nearly back on the phone when he put the brakes on and slid the phone to his ear.

"Ellen? God, Ellen." Josh could barely choke out the words. "What's wrong, sweetheart?"

Her voice had been a mere wisp, the silence that followed so long and drawn out. Josh was reaching for his pants, his shirt, ready to go to her in half a breath if she needed his help.

"I—Josh, don't worry. I'm sorry if I scared you. There's nothing's wrong. At least I—I just needed to talk to you, to explain some things. Could you come over? Or—maybe you'd rather that I come there."

Josh ran a hand along his jaw, tried to still his breathing. Either suggestion sounded like heaven. Neither of them was wise. She was all right. Just some simple talk, some explanations. Ellen was probably feeling silly now that this was over, she was no doubt a bit self-conscious, wanting to clear the air. She probably felt that she needed to set some things straight after the way he had latched on to her today. Maybe she was worried that he'd show up on her doorstep again someday uninvited.

He could assure her that she needn't be concerned about that. He would be able to control himself once he put some space, a few thousand miles, a major body of water between them. Hell, at least he *hoped* he could control himself. He would do his damnedest, but if he went to her right now—no, he couldn't be that big a fool. He just couldn't be sure he'd be able to stand there and conceal the fire that was blazing within him. It would take every ounce of determination he had and then some to disguise the love that was surging through him. There was no way he could go to her like this. None whatsoever.

"Give me ten minutes. I'll be there," he told her, clicking the receiver down in its cradle.

For twenty whole seconds Josh sat there with his eyes closed, struggling for control, praying that he could play the role he needed to play one more time, and that he could let her go without sending her off on some guilt trip that never, ever had been her fault. He was the one who was so in love he could barely drag air into his body. She need never know that; he wouldn't want her ever to know that. This was one problem Ellen Rhoades couldn't fix. She was not responsible for his heart—or his heartache.

He was reciting those last words like a litany by the time he finally made it to her door. The woman was going to drive him certifiably insane if he didn't leave town soon. He was never going to be the same man he had been. He was never going to *want* to be the same man he had been.

The knowledge kicked him just as Ellen swept back the door and pulled him inside.

She stared up at him, smiling, beaming in her long white gown that covered her so completely. No matter, he was pretty darn sure of what was under that gown. He was dead certain that he wanted what was there. And he knew for a fact that if he didn't push his hands into his pockets right now that he was going to reach out and slide his fingers through her long, loose hair. With absolutely no encouragement at all, he'd be lifting her into his arms, he'd be whispering all of the secrets of his soul to her.

Josh stood up straighter. He shoved his hands into his back pockets so far that he could feel the slight popping of threads as they broke. Who cared? He'd sacrifice a thousand pairs of pants if he could just get out of here without scaring Ellen again.

"Hi there," he said gently as she continued to stare at him as if he'd just discovered the secret of world peace. "I—oh hell, Ellen. You needed me. I'm here," he whispered, giving up and freeing one hand to slide it up the soft contours of her face.

She leaned into his touch slightly—or was that just his imagination, just the wanting that had become a part of him?

"I needed to see you one last time." Her voice was rich and low. In another time and place those words could offer heaven to a man.

Josh nearly groaned. He lowered his hand. "I shouldn't be here, with you like this, Ellen. You know damn well it's true."

She froze at his words, her eyes widened slightly

with…uncertainty? Josh cursed his impetuous words, even if they *were* true.

"You didn't want to come," she said simply, suddenly backing away and leaving some space between them. "Josh, for once I want to know. What *do* you really want?"

What did he want? He wanted things he couldn't have.

"Nothing," he said curtly. "Not a thing. But you do. You called me," he reminded her. And he was hoping with all his might that she hadn't called him for the reason that was dawning in his muddled brain. Ever since he'd stepped back into her life, she'd been trying to thank him, to repay him for some perceived debt. She *knew* without any question that he desired her, and now here she was, nearly naked, asking what he wanted. He wanted, sweet heaven, he *wanted*—but no way in hell would he allow himself to take the gift.

Ellen shifted from one bare foot to the other, staring up at Josh's suddenly shuttered expression. She felt exposed beneath her loose gown. She wondered what he thought of her, greeting him this way. Things had seemed so simple when she'd first rushed to the phone. All her plans were tied up with launching herself into Josh's arms, spilling her heart to him as soon as he came close.

But he'd been wary from the moment he stepped through the door. He'd said that he hadn't wanted to come.

Suddenly her plan seemed self-serving, greedy. She'd thought that opening her heart to him was the right thing to do. She'd hoped that he would understand that she wasn't asking for anything in return, but, maybe she'd been wrong. Would her love be an embarrassment? A burden? Would he understand?

She had to try. And so Ellen tilted her head, boldly

staring up at him. She took one small step closer to the man, touched his lips with the fingers of one hand as if to feel the words he wasn't saying.

His body tensed, he nearly closed his eyes, but she wouldn't let him. She held his gaze and took another step forward. Her breasts were nearly against his chest. She had to tip her head back so that she could look at his face. And she wanted very much, she *needed* to see what was written on that face.

"For the past two weeks, Josh, you've been my fairy godfather, my knight in shining armor. You came without my asking, you gave without requiring payment in return. We've had this conversation before," she whispered, stroking her fingers along his jawline. "And now you're leaving, maybe for forever," she added, swallowing hard, trying not to think about how long forever was. She couldn't think that now. She couldn't do as she intended if she gave in to the sharp pain that went with such thoughts.

"I can't let you go without giving you what little I have to offer." Ellen rose on bare toes to brush her lips across his unshaven cheek.

She could feel the breath filling Josh's chest as he sucked in air and held it. His eyes were closed, his jaw tense as he placed his fingers on her arms and held her back.

"Ellen, please, I've told you before that I don't want *anything* from you."

She closed her own eyes against the pain. His words hurt even though she was sure that wasn't his intent. But...forcing her chin back up, returning her gaze to his, she thought—she was almost certain—that he was lying.

"Josh," she whispered, leaning forward even as he held her away. "Don't you believe in the things that you taught me? Didn't you just convince me that it was best to lay my cards on the table? Why aren't you doing the same?''

This wasn't fair. She knew her own heart so well, and she was fully prepared to offer it without thought of reparation. But this was a man who had spent his childhood *never* getting the things that he most wanted and needed. How could she expect him to take his own good advice now, to reach out and demand something for himself?

She waited.

The words ''I love you,'' were there, ready to be said. She wanted to say them, she could easily do so, but *this time* Josh needed to be the one to reach out and ask for…something for himself. If he only would.

They stood there so long, the silence seemed to become a part of them. Somewhere in the distance, a clock ticked away loudly.

She must have been wrong. She was pressuring him, maybe even embarrassing him.

Deep disappointment swirled within Ellen, nearly making her stagger. She curled her fingers under into her palms, drawing back from him. Looking to the side, she struggled to regain what little composure she could.

''Forgive me,'' she began. ''I thought I could—''

A groan slid from Josh's lips. ''Don't, Ellen,'' he said, turning his back to her as he moved to put ten good feet of space between them. ''Don't get down on yourself just because you've failed to repay the blasted debt you seem to think you owe me. And don't you dare spend the rest of your life thinking I'm some honorable so-and-so who was too good to want anything. You, better than anyone, know that I'm a long way from sainthood. And the truth is, dammit, that you're right. I'm not living by the same code I've bullied you into living by. If I was, I'd be forced to admit that you're right. I *do* want something, but there's no way in hell that I'll hurt you by asking you for it.''

A series of shivers went through Ellen. She felt the sting of tears at the back of her eyes as she looked at Josh's strong, proud back.

''Ask.'' She choked out the word.

He turned. His jawline looked like granite, cold and hard and immovable. ''No.''

But she had gone too far to turn back now. Padding across the room, her bare feet brushing against the carpet, Ellen stopped inches away from where Josh stood with his back against the wall. She almost wanted to smile. Her sexy, flirtatious warrior was her prisoner now. He could go no farther.

''Why won't you ask me for something?'' she said, her quiet voice breaking the stillness, demanding a response.

Josh swallowed audibly. He leaned his head back against the wall, but it was clear that her insistent interrogation was getting to him. When he looked down on her, there was a spark in his eyes. He looked angry, dangerous again. The old Josh, the one who'd teased her into loving him against her will.

''Because, sweet lady,'' he said. ''If I told you what I really want, my lovely Ellen, you would give it to me. That same, misguided sense of fairness that you practice on the world would convince you to try to give me whatever I want, even if it isn't in your best interests.''

Josh leaned farther down, closer, daring her to deny his words.

''Are you saying that you think I don't know my own mind?''

"I'm saying that you would ignore your own heart for my sake."

So he thought she would give herself to him out of gratitude? The mere goodness of her soul? Without love, without caring?

"That sounds like you don't have a very high opinion of me," she said, settling her hand on her hips as if she was braced for battle. Suddenly Ellen wished that she was dressed in a power suit.

Josh groaned. "I have the highest opinion of you, but—"

"But you think I'm so eager to please that I will sacrifice myself just to give you what you think you want? Haven't you learned anything about me by now, Josh Hawthorne?" she asked, crossing her arms. "Didn't I march into Hugh Tarenton's office? Didn't I, *before* you even came, take things into my own hands? I do know what I want and I do go after it, Josh. Don't you see that?"

She stood there, fighting the fullness in her heart, waiting, frowning at the man she loved heart and soul.

Josh stared at her, studied her and finally a gentle smile reached his lips. "I guess I do see that," he agreed. "And I've always known that you're one formidable lady. You are a capable woman who can make her own decisions, who can handle the truth."

His last words scared her, froze her in place. The truth. What was it, anyway? That this had been a pleasant interlude, but that was all? That he would never be back, ever?

She stood silently, knowing he was ready, at last, to give her his truth. She had to be ready to take it.

"I want something, Ellen. Oh, yes, I do want something from you. And if I could demand anything I wanted, *anything* at all, you'd be in my arms right now. I'd be holding you against my heart.''

A stream of pure joy flowed through Ellen as she crossed those last few inches of space that separated them and wrapped her arms around Josh's waist. She lifted her lips to be kissed.

But Josh didn't kiss her. He pulled her close, stopping with his mouth only a heartbeat away from hers.

Ellen couldn't keep the confusion from her face. She held her breath and waited, willing Josh to hurry. The night would be gone soon.

''I'm not done telling you what I want, Ellen. So listen closely. More than anything I'd like to slip you out of this sweet little gown, feel you naked in my arms and carry you to my bed. But even that's not enough, sweetheart. Because much as I desire you, even though I'm trembling with my need for you, I want you completely. Commitment. Family. The whole bag.''

He lowered his head, nudged her cheek as he dropped kisses on her jaw and nibbled his way up to her lips. His arms came around her tightly.

''I've always loved you, Ellen, and if you come to me, I don't want it to be a game like the ones we've been playing. This time I want forever.''

Tears filled Ellen's eyes and her heart. ''I wouldn't settle for less with you, Josh. I'm not even sure forever will be enough time.'' She snuggled closer and stood on her toes to kiss him back.

''You're a very demanding lady,'' he whispered against her mouth.

Ellen smiled, the sensitive skin of her lips molding to his own.

''That I am, Joshua Hawthorne,'' she whispered, a mere breath away from his beautiful mouth. ''I *am* demanding, because I only want the best. You. I love you, Josh. You're the man I've always loved. The groom I secretly wanted all along.''

A low chuckle broke from Josh's lips as he leaned back, sliding Ellen up along the length of him until they were eye to eye.

''No need for secrets or pretending this time,'' he said, bringing his lips to her own. ''I love *you,* Ellen Rhoades, and it's the real thing. You're mine, sweetheart. For better, for worse, for always.''

*   *   *   *   *

MILLS & BOON®

*M*akes
any time
special

Enjoy a romantic novel from
Mills & Boon®

Presents...™ *Enchanted*™ TEMPTATION.®

Historical Romance™ ⊣**MEDICAL**
ROMANCE™

MILLS & BOON®

Presents...™

WANTED: WIFE *by Stella Bagwell*

Lucas Lowrimore, high-profile playboy, wants a wife—and he's chosen Jenny Prescott. Badly hurt by her first marriage, Jenny has vowed to remain single forever. But as Lucas launches a charm offensive she feels her resistance melting away…

A BRIDE TO HONOR *by Arlene James*

Paul's grandfather had left him little choice: marry a woman he despised or lose the family business. Then he fell for innocent beauty Cassidy Penno and life became a lot more complicated…

HER SECRET PREGNANCY *by Sharon Kendrick*

Gorgeous Marcus Foreman had been Donna's boss and her first lover. But their one night together had been a disaster and the next day he'd fired her. Nine years later, Donna is back—and Marcus is determined to show her how their first night should have been…

MARRIAGE IN PERIL *by Miranda Lee*

Brooke was happily married to wealthy Italian Leonardo Parini—until she overheard a conversation that suggested he was in love with his late brother's wife… However, it was clear that Leo still desired her, so Brooke decided to fight for the man she loved, not by confronting him, but by giving him all he wanted in bed!

Available from 5th May 2000

4 FREE

books and a surprise gift!

We would like to take this opportunity to thank you for reading this Mills & Boon® book by offering you the chance to take FOUR more specially selected titles from the Presents…™ series absolutely FREE! We're also making this offer to introduce you to the benefits of the Reader Service™—

- ★ FREE home delivery
- ★ FREE gifts and competitions
- ★ FREE monthly Newsletter
- ★ Exclusive Reader Service discounts
- ★ Books available before they're in the shops

Accepting these FREE books and gift places you under no obligation to buy, you may cancel at any time, even after receiving your free shipment. Simply complete your details below and return the entire page to the address below. *You don't even need a stamp!*

YES! Please send me 4 free Presents… books and a surprise gift. I understand that unless you hear from me, I will receive 6 superb new titles every month for just £2.40 each, postage and packing free. I am under no obligation to purchase any books and may cancel my subscription at any time. The free books and gift will be mine to keep in any case.

P0EA

Ms/Mrs/Miss/Mr ....Initials.....................................
BLOCK CAPITALS PLEASE

Surname ....

Address ....

....

....Postcode..............................

Send this whole page to:
UK: FREEPOST CN81, Croydon, CR9 3WZ
EIRE: PO Box 4546, Kilcock, County Kildare (stamp required)